Bitterly humorous, Rose contrasts the complacent, ultimately helpless liberalism of the "civilised" with insurgent raw feeling and deprivation: at once savage and compassionate.

Leslie Wilson, Independent on Sunday, Red Tides

Stealth is her weapon, its edge so sharp you feel its effect as it fillets prejudice, indifference, skewering one's compliant imagination...

What collars – perhaps even haunts –my recollection of these stories, is their intimacy, their seriousness, their humour, life tasted in their voices.

Tom Adair, Scotland on Sunday, Red Tides

The stories have a steely rectitude and an uncompromising determination to face down humiliation and inequality ... economical, moral and compassionate.

Elizabeth Young, the Guardian, Red Tides

An assured, integrated, and poetic collection of stories from someone who has developed her story-telling to the highest level ...she knows exactly how to circle around her topic, to avoid the over-direct statement, to leave the central anger and desires – the red tides, in essence – to suggest themselves.

Douglas Gifford, Books in Scotland, Red Tides

Within each story, Rose succeeds in evoking precisely a much larger story ... by balancing, very delicately, universality of emotional context and specificity of place.

The List

Deceptively light, to the extent that you sometimes feel you've only brushed against a story rather than dwelt inside it. Quite the opposite is the case; the dainty morsels she offers up are effective because they are so sketchy, tempting the reader to speculate, which is when tail brings to sting.

Daniel Cairns, The Observer, Red Tides

Many of Rose's characters face impossible choices, but her unity of vision does not lead to a narrow or repetitive collection. On the contrary, the stories are wonderfully far-ranging.

Margot Livesey, Times Literary Supplement, War Dolls

The short story form, with all its power of suggestion, penetration and distilled insight, is Dilys Rose's medium. Her sketches of moments and scant, isolated fragments in a person's life, burn with details pregnant in their mundanity or strangeness.

Ruth Hedges, The List, Lord of Illusions

Lord of Illusions offers an insightful exploration, by one of Scotland's best short story writers, into the complexities of everyday life shot through with unexpected or chilling revelations.

The List

All Dilys Rose's writing is distinguished by economy, empathy and a sly wit.

Catherine Lockerbie, The Scotsman, Pest Maiden

In Dilys Rose's graceful and elliptical fiction, the mundane reality of everyday life is often a kind of spiritual and intellectual prison... Hovering like a mirage in the background of her work, sometimes revealing itself to be the more substantial structure, is the presence of 'abroad', the world outside and over the sea, where some of her characters manage to escape and yet are unsurprised to discover that their sense of blankness or vague disappointment has followed them too.

Richard W. Strachan, Scottish Review of Books

Also by Dilys Rose

Novels
Unspeakable
Pelmanism
Pest Maiden

Short Stories
Selected Stories
Lord of Illusions
War Dolls
Red Tides
Our Lady of the Pickpockets

Poetry
Stone the Crows
Bodywork
Lure
Madame Doubtfire's Dilemma

SEA FRET

Short Stories

By

DILYS ROSE

Scotland Street Press
EDINBURGH

First Published in the UK in 2022 by
Scotland Street Press
100 Willowbrae Avenue
Edinburgh EH8 7HU

A CIP record for this book is available from the British Library.

ISBN 978-1-910895-62-7

Typeset and cover design by Antonia Shack, Edinburgh
Cover artwork ©Dilys Rose

Printed and bound by Clays Ltd.

Contents

Are you sure
you want to talk to me?

The big guy ahead of me, with body odour which punches above its weight and a T-shirt bearing the rollicking slogan *Murderers' Row*, lollops against the aisle seats and squeezes towards the back of the bus.

You retract your legs. I stuff my bag under the seat and settle down beside you. It's the only empty seat apart from the one which the big guy is aiming for. If we're both careful we won't have to make too much physical contact, though this is no luxury coach. After your casual opener about having already travelled over three thousand miles by bus on this trip – three thousand miles! – you can still opt for silence. Considering the distance you have already covered, your ability to maintain a neutral tone is impressive, though you roll your bus ticket back and forth like a cigarette you're itching to smoke, and murmur about making your final connection.

Are you sure you want to talk to me? The thing is, if you

do, I will pay closer attention than you might expect. Or want.
When you repeat the number of miles you've already chalked
up, I note your red-rimmed eyes, like scallops prised apart
with a shucking knife. After already four days in transit, why
don't you just press your face into the donkey jacket which
doubles as a pillow and doze away the hundred miles we'll
spend in close proximity?

Before departure, the bus driver instructs us, for the
benefit of other passengers, to silence our electronic
equipment and wrap up our phone conversations. He takes
his time over the announcement, relishing his moment of
glory, his power of office and entitlement to intimidate. If he
had a mind to it, his deep, assertive voice suggests, he could
leave us stranded at some nebula of nowhere, the rain falling
steadily on our heads and not a soul on the road finding the
pity in their hearts to stop and offer us a ride. When we are
all chastened and muted, the driver's heavy gold bracelets clink
against capable wrists, he buckles up and power steers us out
of town.

Like the driver I am all for a quiet ride but it's not going to
happen. Not that you are loud, no, you're soft-spoken, low
key and unsmiling so I can't comment on the condition of your
teeth but doubt you have a decent deal on dental insurance.
Which reminds me of a story I heard the other day. In a
country still picking itself up from its time under the Soviet
hammer, a poet was tipped for the Nobel Prize for literature.
Anticipating glorious photo opportunities and not wishing
to be shown up as the poor man of Europe, the authorities
decreed that the man's teeth should be fixed by the state,
so that he could smile widely and evenly when the flashbulbs
popped.

Work commenced but at some point during the drilling,

the filling, the crowning and bridging, news got out that the poet had been pipped at the post by a writer from a wealthier country with, we can probably assume, noticeably better dental treatment. The orthodontic work was halted, leaving the Nobel manqué with a half-gleaming, half-crumbling folly of a mouth. I don't tell you this story. I can't be sure it would make you smile.

You say you are going to visit family who live upstate somewhere. I don't know the place but the name is familiar: an old name transported from the old country, on a brisk clipper or a rackety coffin ship. I imagine it's a rural area though not in any plush, lush way: more hard-pressed dirt than prime real estate; peeling wood shingles; a porch stacked to the eaves with a guilt trip of recycling and several generations of machine parts which might but never do come in handy. There will be animals: a tick-ridden mutt or an edgy, loose-jointed hound; a slink of feral cats in knee-high grass; a snake coiled in the basement like a garden hose, to keep down the rodents. This may be nothing at all like where you're going but this is what happens: you tell me stuff and I make up the rest.

Your hair is the warm, woody colour of a field mouse. You are by no means wee or sleekit or cowran, but perhaps there is something tim'rous about you. You haven't seen your family for several years and plan to spend a month out east. The prompt for your visit is an aged, ailing grandma who may not last another winter. As it is barely spring and the greening of the trees has been held back by recent storms, floods and prolonged low temperatures – attributed to the cloud of volcanic dust which has already spread around most of the world – you are thinking ahead. Going while the going has a purpose.

This is not your first trip back. You've done the journey

several times. Had you flown, you'd have earned enough
air miles for a freebie but no such reward is offered to the
frequent bus traveller. And even though you've dozed on the
coach or passed restless nights on waiting-room benches,
pushing down the crap fast food which is all that's to be had,
your budget is already strained. Not that you put it like that.

Cost a lotta money, you say, a lotta money.

The mention of money so soon makes me wonder if this
might be your lead-in to a sob story, if you'll wind up hitting
on me for a tap. Have you been doing a similar number on
each stage of your trip – bending an ear, elaborating or editing
details as you saw fit? I don't think so. Wouldn't you at least
have mastered the name of your grandma's illness?

It's not eczema, you say. She been on oxygen for two
years. I ain't dumb, you add, then break off and gaze out at the
bare trees and the slip-slide of yellow earth. High above the
highway, without the need of a single wingbeat, a hawk turns
a slow circle. And another. The sky is piebald, a drab blue
daubed with dark, uncertain cloud. You flatten out your bus
ticket. From days of handling, the inkjet printout is beginning
to smudge. You ask to borrow my pen, draw on the back of
your ticket.

My house, you say, holding up an archetypal kindergarten
dwelling: a block topped with a triangular roof, four windows,
a door with a handle, a scribble of smoke spiralling from the
chimney.

And this is me, you say, pointing to a stick person floating
stiffly in mid-air. Ain't no good at drawin.

As with most life stories, the order of your telling is
roundabout, repetitive, full of holes. Your immediate concerns
are grandma's advanced age and infirmity, and meeting up,

after an absence, with the extended family. Your tone remains deadpan, dispassionate, conveys not the slightest hint of anticipation. You don't say, for example, that you can't wait to see your mother, your aunt Pearl, cousin Rodney, are just longing to rock in your arms the new baby of your second cousin. On the subject of new arrivals you are adamant:

Ain't mindin nobody's baby unless there's a emergency involving the hospital. Or somebody pays me to babysit.

Though I've known you for less than an hour, this sounds rehearsed.

Ain't no good with babies. I've applied for a programme in Culinary Arts Plus. Know what I mean by Arts Plus?

You outline the programme content: how many hours of this or that, each possible step of a possible career ladder, in what quickly becomes tedious detail. It's as if your brain holds blocks of information, to be retained and retrieved exactly as given. You reel off the layout of the building in which each class will take place; where cake decoration sits in relation to cooking a charity meal for two hundred or working in a pizza joint; exactly how much you have to pay for meals at the college – twenty cents for lunch, twenty cents! – how much financial support you're due because you are disabled – you make vague mention of a bad knee – and how you won't, as a result, have to take on the usual killer shifts of the catering trade.

At your age – forty – it seems late to be starting on a course which at best will offer minimum wage for the first so many years and then, if you're lucky, up the rate a couple more dollars an hour and possibly throw in a slightly nicer, smarter uniform: a canvas hat with the restaurant logo on the brim, epaulettes, a ceramic name tag rather than a plastic one.

There's a reason for the new start. There's always a

reason. I contribute a few anecdotes from my own time in the catering trade but you don't pick up on anything. We say stuff to each other, offer each other statements about ourselves but don't really get any dialogue going.

That's the turnpike, you say, indicating a sign on the highway. It means we've crossed the state line.

Crossing the state line sounds more dramatic than merging with a more or less identical stretch of tarmac but after a while a few hills rear up, small ponds glint darkly, a broad slow river cuts through the valley. Little about the scenery interests you until we pass a monumental angel standing not far from the road.

Musta been a graveyard there, you say. My grandma's got a graveyard on her land. She got a memorial stone for a girl named Thankful Williams. Twenny-five when she died. Dunno what she had to be thankful for.

With no glimmer of a smile at the sad irony of Thankful Williams but a stolid confidence in your facts, you talk for a while about graveyards and the Civil War, how important it was for a family to bring their young men and women home, to bury their dead in familiar soil. When you dry up on graveyards, I ask whether the state you've travelled from is very different from where you are going.

It's a different shape. State I'm in now is nearly a square. A propos of nothing you pull up the sleeve of your T-shirt and point out a nasty bruise. A woman attacked me the other day. One street over from where I live. I didn't do nothin to her, was mindin my business but she hadn't taken her meds. I musta been in her way and she lashed out. Police say she'll be okay if she takes her meds but me, I won't be walking down that street no more.

The bus bounces along. The view is pretty much as it's

been for the last half hour.

I'm going to sleep for a bit, I say.

You go right ahead.

Nudge me if I snore.

I'd be the last person to care.

I close my eyes, to give you a chance to keep the rest of your story to yourself, and to decide whether I want to hear any more of it. The motion of the bus rocks me into a doze. I jolt awake when the guy in the *Murderers' Row* T-shirt rumbles down the aisle.

Is the big guy asking about transfers? you ask. Maybe I should ask about my transfer. I didn't catch what the driver said at the last stop.

No talking to the driver while the bus is in motion! the driver tells the big guy, loud enough for everybody else to get the message.

The big guy growls and lumbers back up the aisle, head jerking like there's a hornet in his ear. The driver rattles his bracelets, switches on the fan.

I hope we don't run into traffic, you say. I been snarled up in traffic a few times already. Almost missed my last connection.

You check your ticket again, turn it over, study the house on the back, make the stick person flitter about.

My daughter will be twelve tomorrow and I won't be there for her birthday. I missed the last six birthdays. She don't stay with me no more. She's with her father. And his new girlfriend. I had to give her up. For adoption and ... and now I don't get to see her no more. When she's sixteen, I'm pretty sure it's sixteen, she can come see me. If she wants to. Long as I ain't a convicted felon. If I ain't got in no trouble with the law. If I try to see her before that, even just to give her a birthday present,

the new girlfriend will call the cops. And then I won't get to
see my daughter for even longer. The new girlfriend lies about
me. Tells bad lies. Real bad lies. But she's right about one
thing. Ain't no good with babies ... In four years I should have
finished Culinary Arts Plus and likely I'll have a job, maybe in a
pizza parlour, and I'll be able to visit my daughter –

That's a long time to wait.

I dunno about the pizza parlour. I get a lotta pain. My knee.
And I don't always see things right. I ain't dumb.

With only about fifteen miles to go we hit a tailback.
Defying the driver's instructions, people on the bus begin to
fiddle with phones, iPods, electronic games.

If you add up all the trips home I done, you say, it must be
over thirty thousand miles.

Thirty thousand miles – you could have travelled right
round the world!

I guess. There's forms I haveta fill in for the college. I don't
like forms.

Useta get all kindsa forms from the clinic and the school
about my daughter but they got me mad, the forms got me
real mad. So I didn't fill them in. I looked at them and then ...
I haveta fill in all kindsa forms for Culinary Arts Plus. I ain't
dumb.

You give me a sharp look, and suddenly we are too
close for comfort, close enough to see each other's pores,
blemishes, stray hairs, to feel the heat from each other's
breath and it's as well we're at the front, near the assertive
driver, who surely wouldn't allow anything bad to happen on
his shift. But I can't help wondering what's behind that sharp,
dark look in your eyes. I was wrong about tim'rous. You're far
from tim'rous.

Hyperact. Filling in forms makes me hyperact and ... and

then the meds, the meds ... I ain't dumb but I ain't no good with babies neither.

There are holes in your story. Sinkholes.

The tailback opens out, the driver resumes his previous speed and everyone on the bus settles back into passive mode.

Nearly there, I say. And only a few minutes' delay after all. We should make our connections.

I sure hope so. If I don't make my connection, I dunno where I'm gonna sleep tonight. Ain't got money for no motel.

Again it crosses my mind that this might be a hint for a hand-out but you don't pursue it, the bus arrives more or less on time, the driver unlocks the hold and we retrieve our luggage in a brisk and orderly fashion. Your final bus is ready and waiting, its engine running. We say goodbye, wish each other luck. No smiles, no handshakes.

You will remember next to nothing of me – perhaps the colour of my hair, my light Anglo-Saxon eyes, the name of my homeland, my quaint, queer accent. We haven't exchanged names and your lack of curiosity about your travelling companion will afford me, if not you, some protection.

My train is standing on the platform. It's due to depart shortly and already fairly full. I drape my coat over the vacant seat next to me, hoping to keep it vacant and have a quiet journey, when you, the big guy from the bus, sweating from the exertion of hoisting yourself up two tall steps and negotiating your girth with the doorframe, stop and say:

Is this seat free? Going all the way to New York City?

All the way, I reply, hoping this will prompt you to look elsewhere for a seat.

Me too! you say, plumping down and overflowing into my space. Well, hey, we can get acquainted. You were on the coach, right? Man, that was some goddamn quiet journey. I was just thinking to myself all the way and you know what I was thinking? I was thinking, hey, I really wanna talk. Some stuff I been carrying around way too long, you know. Gotta get some stuff out, share it around, know what I'm saying? And hey, we got plenny time to get acquainted. I mean, sometimes you wanna be quiet and sometimes you just gotta tell somebody your story, right?

In a few hours, if the train runs on time and no unexpected delays occur at the airport, I will fly over the Statue of Liberty and under the cloud of volcanic dust which for the last week has brought air traffic throughout much of the world to a standstill. I will fly – unless the volcano spits out more dust, or its bigger more dangerous cousin wakes from his slumber and wants a piece of the action – towards my own story, its gaps and elisions, its traplines and sinkholes, its random acts of violence and love. In the meantime, Mr *Murderers' Row*, are you sure you want to talk to me?

Kiss and Cry

Fen Ha is not doing any kissing, though she could have done
with a hug or a kind glance more than the humped cold
shoulder of her coach, and his awful hawking, that looks and
sounds as if he is trying to sick up a long-legged toad.

Fen Ha is not doing any crying either. She'd rather slash
her wrists than be caught crying. While she remains in the
viewfinders of the Canons, Nikons and Leicas of the world,
Fen Ha's appalled eyes will remain dry black holes. Not a single
salty drop will well, never mind fall. Her head throbs from the
effort of holding back a deluge.

She has already changed into her tracksuit. When she
eventually gets home, the first thing she will do is destroy
the dress, though it's the most beautiful she's ever worn: the
sweet deep pink of peach blossom, wispy as a spring breeze.
One by one she will wrench out three gross of crystals, rip off
the yards of silk trim, rend each reinforced seam as she replays

each perfect but pointless spin and jump.

No-one will stand in her way. Her parents will not mention the cost of the designer, the fabric, the long trips to fittings, which were as much of a break from practice as her coach allowed in the year leading up to the Games.

Fen Ha is barely into her twenties, an ice virtuosa, but life as she knows it will never be the same again. *An otherwise flawless performance: breathtakingly beautiful, balletic.* All for nothing. There are some falls from which you never fully pick yourself up.

She will carry the shreds of her dress into the yard. The chickens will cluck around her ankles. She will douse the chiffon in petrol, set a match to it. By then her coach will have rediscovered his crinkly, avuncular smile and found himself a new Thumbelina. All that will remain of Fen Ha's glittering career will be a pile of scorched crystals.

Sea Fret

Mabel sits on the caravan steps and blows across a steaming, mid-morning cuppa. Her dragnet glance takes in the entire site, *her* site, and far beyond: the scruffy dunes, the grand sweep of the shoreline, the silver-plated sea, the islands.

The lighthoose is clear as day, pet.

Cuthie doesn't see the lighthouse but knows which way to incline his head without his mam jabbing her fag at the coastline and trailing a coil of smoke. What he sees is thick fog pocked with shifting discs of light: a sea fret with floaters.

As ever Mabel reels off the islands, those she can see and those she can't: Inner Farne, Knock's Reef, the Wide Opens, the Megstone, Staple, the Brownsman, North and South Wames, Big Harcar, Longstone, Knivestone. She skips most of the smaller islands but can list the lot from north to south, west to east, with every tidal coupling and uncoupling. Today she has a hankering and an abbreviated list is all she can be arsed with.

A lighthoose is a landmark.

When Cuthie could first recite the names of all the Farnes, without screwing up or shilly-shallying, she treated him to a plastic, wind-up toy of Grace Darling in her coble. He must have been five or six, not long started at the school and out at last from under her feet. How he'd squealed with glee at wee Gracie rowing like the clappers around the bathtub. How his eyes had grown damp and round with disappointment when the clockwork ran down and the boat puttered to a halt. He played with it so much the mechanism packed up, and the Heroine of the Sea, bobbing about like a rubber duck, just couldn't cut it.

But that's water down the plughole. If Cuthie has forgotten a few of the Farnes, if he's let go of his learning, that's his lookout. High time he learned to take his bearings from what's staring him in the face. You teach a kid something once, you've done your bit. Can't always be filling in the gaps. He chose to stick around, to take advantage of a fully equipped caravan of his own, far enough from hers that he could come and go as he pleased, with a wage on the doorstep into the bargain. A bloody good wage she gives him, a fair hike from what other lads who couldn't be doing with school are taking home.

You need a landmark in your life, Cuth: a goal, a focus, a direction.

Do you have a direction, Mam?

Apart from me stairway to heaven, pet? That would be telling.

She stubs out her fag and kicks the butt off the step. Mabel might keep her van spick and span but isn't fussed about the state of the site. It rained heavily in the night and the pathways have turned to sleck. As if dog do isn't bad enough – and she'll

read the riot act to folk who don't bag and bin the leavings of
their pets – sheep and deer get in through gaps in the fence.
Even cows wander off the dunes and drop their plops of muck
about the place. Sometimes she'll get Cuthie to shovel the
cow-pats into a wheelbarrow and fertilise the tattie patch but
often as not she'll let them lie. Drainage, too, has always been
a problem and after last night's downpour there's no doubt
about it: the site stinks.

She did try. Back in the day, when she first took on the
place, she came down hard on slovens and litter louts but
there's only so much you can do and what, in the long run, is
the point? If folk want to roll in their own muck, why get in a
stew? If they pay the rent on time, or before she has to fetch
Tiff or Nolan to speed up the process, she can sleep easy.
Which is good enough for her.

If truth be told, Cuth –

When his mam gets on to truth-telling Cuthie switches off.
Her philosophy of life is as random as her site maintenance,
though the old fella with the sickle looms large, lurking in the
lee of the dunes, shielding the empty sockets of his eyes from
windblown sand. His mam's nowhere near old and, despite her
bad habits, in rude health. Yet something's forever nipping at
her heels: if she doesn't grab a day by the scruff – except when
it comes to tidying up the site, that is – she's convinced she'll
be jinxed for evermore by missed opportunity.

So clear, she says. Nolan'll be raking it in the day. They'll
be queueing up with their binocs and tripods and all the other
crap twitchers cart aboot. So clear. I reckon you could pick
oot Nolan's boat when it cuts by Inner Farne.

Cuthie can't see the beach, never mind the islands. A sea
fret is all. And floaters. That's what Kyleen in the optometrist's
called the speckles swimming across his field of vision. Wee

and skinny she is, with a pink ponytail, a sparkly nose stud
and a name tag pinned to her shrimpy chest. Diamond, she
said, when he admired the stud. He reckoned it was cubic
zirconium – his mam's addiction to shiny stuff had taught him
to tell the difference – but he wasn't one to challenge a lass.

Kyleen was nice. Didn't gawp when he tried to settle his
lumpy self on the high stool, or titter when his ears caught in
the goggle contraption. She didn't blather on or ask a heap of
questions, just slipped behind her machine and went through
the tests with the lights and the numbers, the rings and dots
and circles. The last test, puffs of air fired at his eyeballs, was
totally freaky.

All done, she said, as he got off the stool, blinking and
bumping against the equipment. Nowt to worry about. But if
you start to see a load o them floaters, come right back and
we'll take a closer look. He wasn't in any rush to have air shot
at his eyeballs again, not even by Kyleen.

He's got a swarm of floaters the day, and a sea fret, and
he's hasn't touched any drugs in a week. He's been trying to
lay off. He's seen enough casualties, doesn't want to turn into
a tottering, toothless wreck before he's out of his twenties.
The floaters are part clear, part cloudy, pulsing like a swarm
of jellyfish when a wave nudges them forward a smidge then
sucks them back. Not a swarm, a smack. A smack of jellyfish.
Uncle Nolan taught him that.

I'm off to see a man aboot a dog, says Mabel. Mind and
wave if you see Nolan's boat oot by Inner Farne.

Nolan couldna see me waving from here, Mam. That's
fancy.

He'd been out in Nolan's boat with his brothers. His uncle
had just started up the Farne Isles trips and had taken Mabel's
boys along for the ride. It was a perfect day for it: sunny,

with a light breeze, the water ice blue, the wind dropped to a ruffle, flashes of sunlight, swathes of lilac cloud, the lighthouse blinding white. They'd seen thousands of birds, a dozen seals. Nolan had given them a pair of binoculars to share but by the time you homed in on a puffin or a seal and faffed with the focus, whatever you'd wanted to see had moved out of the viewfinder.

Aidan is in Dubai, making good money in construction. Comes home every other year, with dutiful duty-free treats. Will is in Sydney, skewering prawns in a harbourside eatery six nights a week, still nattering about getting together the plane fare home. They Skype, now and again, but it's not the same.

Mostly the brothers had squabbled about whose turn it was. That day on the boat, they'd chugged through a smack of jellyfish, a dense reddish-orange variety you could tell packed a punchy sting. There must have been hundreds of them, some just below the surface, others deeper down, some small and thin as communion wafers, others big as bin lids. Cuthie had been hogging the binoculars when Aidan and Will grabbed his ankles and made as if they were going to tip him overboard. He'd blubbed and near wet himself. Nolan had laughed. When the boys got home – they lived in a proper house then – their mam was red-eyed, belligerent and bereft.

Inheriting the site from an elderly aunt didn't turn out to be the golden egg it was cracked up to be but the rent money put food on Mabel's table and three growing boys could get through a trough of grub. Besides, something to call her own meant she could hold her head high when Derek buggered off, chasing his pipe dream of sheep farming in Oz, and the long-legged antipodean tart who had charmed the pants off him.

Mabel has never been married to the idea of constant maintenance: if there's a leak, shove a bucket under it and carry on. Folk rent from her because they'd rather put up with rough and ready, with take what you get or sod off, than pay over the odds. And her cash-only policy suits everybody well enough.

If truth be told, there can be value in clart. Where there's muck and all that. Most mornings, at first light, she makes the rounds of the site, a magpie for jewellery, watches, coins: anything that glints. Then she scours the beach, on the lookout for ancient loot as well as stuff dropped by yesterday's strollers and lollers, trippers and twitchers. It's a fair bet there must be Viking pins, bangles and brooches buried in the dunes or nestling in rockpools as well as tat. There've been plenty of wrecks on the coast, hundreds of years' worth of wrecks and who knows what sunken treasure might shimmy in on the tide.

Thin pickings this morning: a couple of mismatched silver earrings, a gold-plated belly-button stud, a Swatch watch. Mabel has a lost property box in the site office but all she'll ever consign to it are wind-buckled brollies, crusty mobile phones and mouldy swimsuits which nobody ever bothers to claim.

Mind you keep an eye on them neds with the brindle greyhound. They've to clean up after it or they're oot on their arse.

They do clean up, Mam.

No just when it suits them, no just when they've the poop scoop to hand and nowt else demanding their attention. Rain, hail or shine, Cuthie, or they can bugger off.

Aye.

Toodle-oo then, pet. You're me eyes and ears.

Mabel lights up again, checks her watch, wonders what the traffic on the A1 will be like.

When'll you be back?

Sooner or later. Bugger! she says, and a grin splits her face at the effrontery of it: them bloody gulls have crapped all over me windscreen!

She pads across the grass, climbs into the Jeep and roars up the track, wipers slicing a guano-free arc, wheels spraying sleck as she goes.

So, a Tiff day. Cuthie rubs his arms. It's warm but he has goose pimples. What he can see has little form and even less substance: pockets of light and shade in muted tints, oval blobs which he knows must be caravans. His mam's motor is a dark, dwindling smear on a blur of tarmac.

A bee buzzes close to Cuthie's right ear then loops over his head and swings in close. He covers his face with his hands and stays very still. He's allergic to bee stings. A caravan door scrapes open. He hears several pairs of feet galumph down rickety steps then spurts of male laughter. Folk say the blind hear better than the sighted. Cuthie can smell the sleck, the bins, the toilets, the salty rot of the tideline, traces of wildflower sweetness which can't outdo the bad smells. Folk say the blind have a better sense of smell than the sighted. He doesn't want to think about having to sniff his way around.

The lads must have started up some kind of game and the dog's excited barking suggests that something is being thrown around: a ball, a stick, a Frisbee, though Cuthie wouldn't put the lads down as Frisbee types. Was it yesterday or the day before when he last saw them, when his sight had been clear? Whenever it was, he hadn't paid close attention; it didn't do to stare at folk too closely or more to the point, to be seen staring.

Cuthie's not much of a dog lover, nor is his mam. Tiff is forever on at her to get herself a dog, for some clout when she needs it. Officially Tiff is a dog breeder but makes his real money from pharmaceuticals. The kennels are cover, and insurance. Tiff specialises in Staffies: a stocky, rock-headed breed with a capacity for viciousness and, around Tiff's bit, a reputation for it.

A couple of years back, when the brothers were still buddies, Nolan and his wife Tammy had gone to eat with Tiff and his current squeeze. Was that Carmen, or Svetlana? Against Nolan's advice, Tammy had insisted on taking Cream Puff along. Tammy took her toy poodle everywhere, even into the lav. Nobody was going to stop her taking him to her brother-in-law's. Tiff swears to this day that he warned Tammy that his house dogs, Trex and Marge, were full-on territorial. Perhaps Cream Puff, tricked out in ribbons and bows, was too wired to sit nice on Tammy's lap, or his scrabbly claws were doing damage to her leather mini-skirt. Whatever, Tammy let him off the leash to nose around. While the four got stuck in to Tiff's industrial-strength Margaritas, Cream Puff pranced across the shag-pile and out through the open French windows.

It was very quick, according to Nolan, a minute tops, before Tiff's bruisers accosted the dainty canine trespasser. By the time Tiff had set down his drink on the smoked glass coffee table and gone to investigate the eruption of snarls and snaps and pitiful yelps, it was all over for Cream Puff: his neck was broken and his wee curly head mauled something terrible.

Tiff put the poodle out of his misery with a single shot to the head, gave Trex and Marge a leathering and locked them up for the rest of the night. Tammy was beside herself. Dinner was abandoned. The brothers and their respective women haven't spoken since. These days, if Mabel needs a heavy hand on the site, one brother at a time is all she can get, which is a deal less persuasive than both together.

The brindle greyhound continues to bark but in a more muted, experimental manner and the laughter gives way to a conspiratorial murmur. The lads appear to have regrouped near the path to the beach, at least Cuthie thinks that's where they are, but he's guessing. He can't even be sure how many they are as their shadows keep overlapping. How could he possibly see to it that they clean up after the dog?

They must have heard Mabel leave. They must know he's alone. He knows they're watching him, he can sense it, staring long and hard. What he doesn't know is whether they're just bored, daft lads or proper neds. He should have paid more attention when they first arrived. When he could see. He should have watched how they were with each other, checked for signs of weapons, should have eavesdropped on the talk when they were hanging around the barbecue pit. Got the measure of them through their talk.

Mabel pulls into the yard, parks her Jeep around the back of the house. She lights up and makes her way to the barn where Tiff takes care of business. If folk are buying dogs, they might be treated to a snifter in his Poggenpohl kitchen but drug punters rarely get over the door of his home. If they need to take a slash or puke, they can use the outside lav.

As she passes the kennels, a dozen dogs, in a frenzy of barking, hurl themselves against the mesh of their cages. Mabel stiffens, then quickens her pace; she's always jangled by the dogs. Strains of 'Voodoo Chile' escape from the barn. Tiff's taste in music has always been old school. Mabel grinds the fag butt into the gravel and raps the pass code on the door, eagerly anticipating her big bad brother's box of tricks.

Getting to his own caravan at the far end of the site is out of
the question. Cuthie feels his way up the steps of his mam's
van, goes inside and bolts the door. To prevent a bollocking
later for trailing mud across the carpet, he kicks off his trainers
then inches through the kitchen area, feeling for the fridge, the
washing machine, the cooker. There are times when he'd like
a bit more space between himself and the units but today he's
thankful for the snug fit, and his mam's attention to detail –
everything flush, no sharp edges, no obstacles at any level – is
close on miraculous. He was an idiot to let her go off and leave
him.

In the living area, after checking for anything untoward and
feeling only the velveteen upholstery, he flops down on the
sofa-bed and buries his face in a cushion smelling of fag smoke
and peachy air freshener. It's hot. He'd open a window but a
bee might get in. Indoors, the sea fret has a yellow tinge but
fewer floaters. It could be some kind of weird comedown.
He should have asked his mam. Should have said something,
dreamed up some gambit to postpone her trip to Tiff's, though
he'd have had to come up with a hell of a good one.

He rolls over until he's flat on his back. The sofa-bed
creaks. The fridge clanks and rumbles. His pulse thumps. Do
the lads with the greyhound know his mam keeps the rent
money in the caravan and only banks it once a week? Do they
know she won't be back for hours – and maybe not until the
following morning? His breath crashes against the caravan
walls. The Xpelair whirs and clicks. Outside, a bee, buzzing
angrily, bumps against the window. And is that the dull thud of
a bunch of neds approaching, is it the low growl of a brindle
greyhound – muzzle wrinkled, lips retracted, teeth bared?

Overlookeringstraat

Regarding the neighbourhood, Rona does her homework too late. Arriving ahead of the agreed meeting time with the agency rep, she kills the spare time in a canalside bar. It's a dirty, desolate place. Marine-themed junk is festooned with cobwebs thick as ropes, the barman gives her a far from friendly onceover, posters on the wall carry violent slogans amidst clenched white fists. The window overlooks a *pissour*, a curved metal urinal which barely covers the groins of a steady stream of not so steady guys. Rona won't be frequenting the local.

On the way to the apartment, her eye is caught by a street-level window suffused with a deep red glow and plush curtains; very stagey and late-night for a Sunday afternoon. Rona is wondering what the curtains might conceal when a woman in complicated underwear parts the curtains and smiles out – at her! Rona returns the smile and is raising a hand to wave when it clicks: she blushes, blinks and scurries round the corner, the wheels of her heavy suitcase rumbling and bumping. In town half an hour and solicited by one of the world-famous *hoertjes!*

On a previous visit to the city, she'd accidentally wandered into the blare, the glare and tacky sleaze of the official red-light district, where everything from keyrings to roadside bollards resembles sexual organs and XXX has nothing to do with the Heroism, Steadfastness and Compassion proclaimed on the city's coat of arms.

It wasn't her intention to rent anywhere near the red-light district. According to her map, she isn't in it and these quiet little canalside alleys don't match her memory of the XXX experience. Perhaps the woman – if it *is* a woman – is a one-off, a free spirit who has set herself up in business off the beaten track? That wishful thinking only lasts as far as the crossroads: to the left is the church she was told to look out for; to the right, a stone's throw from her door, an alley decked out with quaint but decidedly rosy-hued lanterns.

From the tiny, cracked skylight in the tiny toilet under the eaves, Rona sees, through grime-speckled glass, a purple door opening onto an external staircase which appears to be suspended in mid-air. A woman in a fur hat, wool coat, winter boots and a festive red scarf, drags out a bag of rubbish, secures it between two large potted plants, pulls the door to, then clicks down the stairs and out of sight.

Above the rooftops, the sky is an overloaded palette of steel, pewter and leaden hues which shift, swill, dissolve. Another level up, framed by a square window, a caged yellow bird hops from perch to perch. Goldfinch! she thinks, though she's pretty sure it's a canary. The cage quivers.

This is a shaky city, built on peat bog, embraced by canals.

Developments for the new metro system are causing havoc with the foundations of buildings which date back to the Golden Age. Somewhere out of sight a high-pitched drill rips through the afternoon. As she negotiates the rickety toilet seat, Rona tries to calculate angles of incidence from skylight to purple door or window with yellow bird. Which parts of her might be visible – knees, thighs, the lot?

The sleeping area of her apartment has room only for a double bed and two wonky bedside tables. A black blind covers the wide window. Even with the lights on the space is dark and the bed has a severe, wrought iron frame, better suited to bondage than to relaxation. She rolls up the blind and damp, grey light seeps in. Several nearby windows now overlook her unmade bed and, as she'd taken a nap after the agency girl pushed off on her bike, her undressed self. At one window, a heavily tattooed man paces, smokes a fat cigar, jaws down the phone and jabs the air for emphasis. At another, a sumptuous African woman leans through the open casement and snaps dust from a rug. How many windows overlook her rented bed?

When she asked about the neighbourhood, the very young, very pretty but not very well-informed girl showed her on the map just how near and easy to find the red-light district was.

I'm not actually wanting to find it, Rona said.

At this point the rep's English deserted her and, having got what she'd come for – the credit card payment and a whopping damage deposit – she made a hasty exit.

In a country known for an overabundance of sky, little is visible. At the front of the Benedictus apartment, named after the church opposite and affording the apartment an undeserved aura of tranquillity, a massive wall runs the length of the alley. Though it blocks out the sky, the wall has compensations: the soothing umbers and ochres of seasoned brick, the green moss furring the mortar. But more to the point, no-one can see in to her living room.

Well, no-one who might be in the church. Where the wall meets the crossroads, another batch of windows faces her own. At street level, glass-fronted on two sides, as devoid of charm or comfort, as functional as an auto-repair shop, is the office-cum-waiting room of a brothel. Two men, both shaven-headed, stubble-chinned, dogged, clatter out onto the street, throwing punches and insults, circling each other in a belligerent ring-a-rosy. Rona doesn't understand the language but the tone translates, as does the hike in decibels. Passersby – kids on bikes, women negotiating with grocery bags, backpackers in search of 'coffee bars' and crash pads, and a loose string of solo men, hands in pockets, checking out the window displays – side-step the disturbance and continue on their way.

Two floors up are more of the big, plain, practical windows. For four hundred years, furniture was hoisted up the exterior walls and swung through open casements – and still is: for the purpose, a sturdy, ancient hook swings on the other side of the glass. Rona can see straight onto somebody else's rumpled bed. A pair of red stilettos pokes through the duvet and an empty bottle stands on the bedside table, double-cupped by a red bra. Otherwise, the room is stark, clinical, the light harsh, the kind of light you might want for deep cleaning, for routing things out of corners. The door opens onto a shadowy hallway.

At another window a man and woman are eating lunch. The bread is round and golden brown, the cheese creamy with a burnt orange rind, the crockery blue. The room is warmly lit, its furnishings earth-toned. The woman pours wine into the man's glass, her gaze trained on the ruby stream between bottle and glass.

Vermeer! Rona exclaims, but with a touch of irritation. Peace and privacy are what she paid for – and paid over the odds – only to find herself in a triple X satellite, and overlooked in every direction. Still, even in nicer parts of town, Amsterdammers have always overlooked each other, always had an eye pressed to the glass, an ear to the wall.

The drilling persists. Rona edges down the stairs; the treads are so shallow she has to turn sideways, and the staircase is so narrow that a very large person could easily get stuck. Have bodies ever been winched up or down the exterior walls? And what about coffins? As she passes the apartment below, the sweet fug of incense and the canned laughter of a gameshow oozes into the stairwell. No name on the door, just a cutesy little sticker featuring a clump of magic mushrooms. Well, what did she expect – sunflowers?

The queue for the Rijksmuseum stretches out of the gate and far around the corner. It has begun to rain. Umbrellas are opened; hoods are pulled down; a cold wind blows. As the museum is packed to capacity, in order for people to enter, some have to leave but Rona's pass allows her to fast track. At the cloakroom she is asked to deposit bag as well as coat and so, pen and notebook in hand, reading glasses on a chain around her neck, in she goes.

Rona has rationed herself to five paintings. No Rembrandts. The Rembrandt room is bound to be chockablock, an echo-chamber of coughs and shuffles, no place for proper thought. First, Carel Fabritius's *Goldfinch*. The Dutch title, *Het Putterje*, as the wall card explains, comes from the bird's trick of being

able to collect water with a bucket the size of a thimble.
Clever bird.

The painting is breathtaking in its simplicity. Just a bird
on a feeder attached to a pale wall, paint applied freely with
a loaded brush, a gold flash on a wing the strongest note of
colour. The soft contours of its body, the cock of its head
suggest movement, vitality but in spite of his teacher's dictum:
Follow life, Fabritius is more likely to have based his subject on
a stuffed specimen than a live finch.

> *Trompe l'oeil? F's illusion of real bird perched high in room also*
> *symbolic attempt to bring the dead back to life?*

The fine chain tethering the bird's leg to the wall bar describes
a loose arc. Rona needs to put on her glasses to see it clearly.
In public, the tools of her trade make her self-conscious. She
takes notes too quickly, shielding her words in the crook of
an arm, like a kid writing a *Strictly Private!* diary. Not that what
she's writing is intended, eventually, to be private – far from it.
She's hoping to gain as wide a readership as possible.

> *Bird chained to feeder a form of social comment or impartial*
> *observation?*

Beautiful, isn't it? Beautiful and sad.

A tall man in a tatty, slate grey outfit stands beside her. A
straggle of grey hair. Watery grey eyes. The smell of drink on
him. Cognac.

All beautiful things are sad.

I could look at that painting all day, says Rona, but the
gallery is only open for another two hours, so I must –

So, you must make the most of your time. Feast on the

many pleasures of the collection –

There are too many for one day.

And you are not only here for pleasure, he says evenly, eyeing her notebook.

It's always good to talk to another art lover, she says.

Ah, no. I am not *art* lover. Well, I go now. Good looking.

He turns on his heel and heads off, crumpled coat swishing, leaving her to *Goldfinch*. Her gaze slides from the bird to the wedge of shadow behind it.

When an Italian study group floods the room with expansive syllables, Rona moves on. In Gabriel Metsu's *The Sick Child,* a child sits on a woman's knee. Though there is great tenderness in the woman's encompassing attitude, the wan child's pose suggests that she can't summon up enough energy to make herself comfortable. The bold primary colours in the clothes only emphasise the child's sickly pallor, the deep shadows around eyes fixed far beyond the viewer, the moment. Beautiful. And sad.

Woman too old to be mother? Grandmother, nanny, neighbour?

On the surface, Pieter de Hooch's work, *A Mother's Duty,* has less emotional pull, is more a marvel of perspective and compositional detail. In the right foreground – and the composition is split down the middle – is an ordinary, domestic scene: a mother checking her child's hair for nits. Art historians have suggested a moral message implicit in the action – combing for sins as well as nits – but Rona is not convinced, not even by the reference to duty in the title.

Subjects not individual enough, little more than figure studies. Stock poses. De H has put his creative energy elsewhere.

On the left, through an open door, in front of which a dog sits, entranced, we move through another room and, via an open window, to the world outside: trees in bloom, sunlit sky. Domesticity gives way to the draw of beyond.

I think de Hooch hit the wall running.

You again!

We walk the same walk. By coincidence or design.

I don't read anything into coincidence, Rona snips.

Ah, but coincidence might read something into *you* – I wanted to tell you my theory about this Pieter de Hooch. When a man gets too caught up in domestic interiors he has to open a door. Open a door and step outside. Or inside. But step somewhere else.

The door de Hooch opened didn't lead to better things.

Are you sure?

Not yet, no.

Ah, he says. But I am interrupting your train of thought – can you say 'tram' of thought? That will never do. I must leave you to your appreciation of Old Dutch Masters. See you around.

Oh, I don't think so –

But I do, he says. This town is a village.

Once again, he departs. For a big man, he is light on his feet, and quick off the mark.

Rona returns her attention to de Hooch, fixes on a diamond of sunlight cast on terra cotta floor tiles.

De H died in madhouse. Find out more about family life, 17th C. treatment of mental illness.

The intensity of blue in the skirt and yellow of the woman's bodice hits Rona from across the room, as if Vermeer had meant the viewers to drink in the colours to the point of intoxication. *The Kitchenmaid* gazes at the creamy flow from jug to bowl. Self-contained, absorbed, possibly preoccupied, she does not in any way invite the viewer's gaze. Caught in this ordinary domestic scene, soft light from the window highlighting forehead, cheekbone, wrist, bodice, cap and skirt, the maid with her workaday features and solid frame is as serene as any Madonna. The skirt, tucked up to keep it clear of a dusty floor, or to reflect a fashion of the period, is a deep pool of blue.

Unashamedly, Rona hogs her spot. At arm's length from the painting, no-one can comfortably cut in front of her, and politeness prevents people nudging her out of the way. The longer she contemplates the still, wholesome scene, the easier it becomes to ignore the bustle of the gallery and the progress of time until a smartly dressed attendant announces that the gallery will close in twenty minutes.

In Jan Steen's *Woman at her Toilet,* the subject sits on her box bed and removes a red stocking. The garter mark on her leg is unmistakeable. Holding her skirt above the knee she flashes a generous expanse of inner thigh. A dappled dog, featured in other paintings by Steen, is asleep on the woman's pillow. On the floor is a used chamber pot and a pair of the heeled, backless slippers often left lying around Old Dutch Masterpieces. Style and symbolism. The woman is engrossed in easing the red stocking over her ankle. She gives no sense of being observed, or overlooked. Except, of course, by Steen. It's a work of intense, voyeuristic intimacy.

Rona scribbles quickly, one eye on the exodus of visitors:

If the dog does represent lust, if the word for stocking, kous,
is a play on female genitalia, and 'darning your stockings' a
euphemism for sex, if pieskous is another word for slut and
if, for three hundred years this woman's thighs were modestly
covered by a white petticoat, it would be difficult not to
interpret the scene as a representation of loose morals. And yet
the woman is painted with such affection: her downcast face,
framed by kiss-curls, so gently absorbed in preparing for bed.
Vulnerability rather than titillation. Who was the model?

As she writes, Rona glances round, half-expecting the man in
grey to reappear, breathe his boozy breath down her neck and
venture another opinion, but the room has been cleared and
the attendant is keen to usher her out.

Daan rakes in his pocket for the key to the street door,
which he was sure he'd left open when he popped out to the
corner shop. Once inside, he leaves the door on the latch.
The intercom's broken and he can't be arsed going up and
down the stairs all evening. He steps over the pile of junk mail.
Further up, a door bangs, a key turns in the lock. The new
tenant is back already. Only been out for what, three or four
hours, when she could have been chilling in a cafe, getting into
the vibe.

   The Benedictus alternates between short rents, city breaks,
dirty weekends and longer rentals, mostly to working girls
trying to set up in business who, sooner or later, usually score
from him. A lot of the time, the tourists are out and about.
There's plenty to keep them trailing round the smoking,
drinking and screwing holes, plenty to keep them out of his
hair but the chick who arrived early in the afternoon and

woke him well before he wanted to surface, seems to have
other things in mind than entertainment or making money. He
heard her bump a heavy suitcase up the stairs, and then, as she
unpacked, the thud of thick books – far more reading material
than anybody normally brings for a city break. He knows what
books sound like: he worked for an antiquarian bookseller for
a bit but it wasn't for him: the fusty smell did his head in, as
did the crusty old punters, fussing about foxing and torn title
pages, browsing for hours then buying zilch.

Daan's bed is directly beneath the bedroom of the
Benedictus and sleep – deep verging on comatose or shallow
and dream-filled – is pretty much his favourite pastime. Sex
is okay now and again, and if he has an itch for one of the
neighbourhood girls, there's always somebody who owes him
a favour. He hears plenty of bump and grind from upstairs,
though by the time the tourists get back from a night on the
town they're usually too off their faces for a fuckathon.

He turns up the gas fire and unpacks his supplies from the
corner shop: tea and coffee, pizza and cookies, tobacco and
papers, bottle of Jack Daniels. When the phone rings, he's
skinning up.

Yeah, he says. Been shopping, man.

He does some weighing and bagging in the kitchen area,
behind a screen on which the Virgin of Guadalupe shakes and
rattles and breaks up into a thousand painted beads. He likes
his business. Keeps his own hours, doesn't need to leave the
house to make a living or have a social life.

Dirk and Otto accept a shot of Jack, make short work of a
joint and are ready to split in less than fifteen minutes. Earlier
in the day they were tearing strips off each other but apart
from a bruise or two are all palsy-walsy again. They didn't say
– and Daan knows better than to ask – but with these guys,

money and girls, in some combination or other, are at the root
of any quarrel. It's good to get the pair of them sorted early
on, to know they won't be back at his door for a while.

His phone rings again.

Yeah, yeah. See you in ten.

He channel-surfs. Are Brits only interested in quiz shows,
ballroom dancing and old guys in fast cars?

The lights in the church across the way are on and two
tall, arched windows glow softly. In one, a knight in armour
defends the Christian faith. In the other, a virtuous woman
casts her eyes heavenwards. Rona finds the muted colours
of the stained glass a soothing counterpoint to the sudden
spills of noise on the street – the brash laughter, the buzz of
scooters zipping down the narrow alley, the intermittent fracas
of broken glass.

Maritsa straightens the bed, throws the beat-up red stilettos
into the pile at the bottom of the wardrobe, picks out an
electric blue pair which go nicely with the new black and blue
basque. She snorts a couple of fat lines and fixes herself a
vodka and Bols Blue. Likes to be colour-coordinated. Still a bit
of time to enjoy the high before her first customer is due.

Across the way, Daan is sprawled on the sofa, as per usual.
Dirk and Otto are settling up, closing their wallets. Lazily,
Daan rouses himself to see them out, a mop of curls falling
into his eyes. Maritsa likes Daan. Cute, passive, easy to please.

The lights are on in the Benedictus. It can't be everybody's
cup of tea, sharing a stair with Daan. Not as if the cops leave
him alone *all* the time and he's far from fussy about who
he does business with. Earlier in the day, the new girl was
hanging around the alley with her suitcase, checking out the

competition, no doubt. A bit long in the tooth but Maritsa
knows there's a market for all sorts. Doesn't look like much,
but you'd walk past plenty off-duty girls on the street. Wigs,
make-up, accessories, where would they all be without the
tricks of their trade?

What she doesn't get is all those big, boring-looking books
stacked up on the dining table Maritsa would love to get her
hands on. If she had a table like that, she'd throw a dinner
party, cook up a storm. What good are books around here?
And backing off from the window like that, perching on a stool
by the frigging cooker with your specs dangling on a chain like
an old schoolmarm? The whole point of windows is to see.
And be seen. To advantage.

Maritsa switches on the UV, transforming her room to a
cavern of dark light. The blue basque throbs like a clutch of
electric eels. Her skin takes on a deep, blemish-free blush. Her
fingernails glow like stars. She downs her drink, adjusts her
stockings. Her first customer, a regular, is on his way. Dodgy,
but always pays over the odds. Amongst other things, he likes
a bit of costume drama. Golden Age caps and gowns. Millstone
collars. Along with a snifter of cognac. Only drinks cognac.
Maybe she'll leave the blinds open. Let the new girl see what
she's up against.

The Blue Beyond

It's a blue day. Soft blue. Blue water, sky, hills, aye the hills are bonny the day and the water flat and smooth as a clean sheet. Seamless. No that, on my shift, I look at the view. I turn my back on the view. And the bus pairties.

The boss disna like my attitude. Says I should get on wi my work, in full view o the veesitors, tip my cap, gie a wee smiley and carry on filletin salmon like I'm on piecework, while they, the veesitors, consult the leaflets that wir pressed upon them at the door. They read aboot how vital the smokehoose is tae oor bonny wee neuk, how they should be proud tae support the local economy and no mind payin ower the odds for premium quality and the distinctive flavour got by smokin fish ower the shavins o auld whisky barrels.

The shop dis a fair enough trade. When folk have been wheeched roond dizzens o blind bends on a single-track road, they're keen tae stretch thir legs and flash plastic at ony kinna retail outlet. And seein me at the filletin is good for sales, the boss says. Pairt o the experience. But the boss is no on the premises the day. He's awa tae the lodge wi a delivery o langoustines for the huntin, shootin brigade, so I keep my back tae the view. And the veesitors.

Some bugger chaps on the windae, hopin I'll turn and oblige wi a cheery, Hielan welcome but I keep the heid doon and my back tae the viewin gallery, keep on slicin through the reid fish flesh, the knife skimmin a fan o banes, the fish scales worryin my epidermis, and the reek playin havoc wi my respiratory tract.

Some bugger chaps on the windae – hopin tae catch a glimpse o the mannie that fillets the salmon, slicin the reid flesh head tae tail, quick as a wink. Hellbent on catchin me on camera, happy at my work, tae bore thir freends wi when the holiday's done.

When I dinna oblige, they move on, snappin shots o the blue beyond – sea, sky, hills, islands – aw hues o the same soft blue. And they sigh, mibbe get a bit weepy, mindin some soft blue view they turned their backs on long ago.

When my shift is done, I dauner hame, in the blue gloamin. Mhairi wrinkles her nose at the reek o me, packs me off tae the shower tae scrub masel raw, afore she'll let me near her.

Correspondence

The boy, in mittens, muffler and woollen cap, shields his eyes against the snow glare and looks down over a city which may never feel like home.

His father is everywhere. Hatless, gloveless, at once intent and distracted, he makes his way along broad, frosty Bahnhofstrasse. In one hand he carries a violin case, in the other a small valise. He still has a good walk ahead of him but appears to be in no hurry: he ambles across the Gemüsebrucke, where the market is in full swing. He pauses at a flower stall and stoops to inspect the roses standing in buckets of water. For the longest time he scrutinises the blooms, compares the scent and colour, the condition of petal, leaf and stalk.

He has just arrived from Berlin on a packed, overnight train. The border, closed for months, was opened briefly and those able to find a space on the train were celebrating their good fortune: the blockade has been causing considerable shortages and as the winter progresses the impact is worsening.

Predictably, there were lengthy holdups while border guards inspected papers. In the way of incident nothing serious occurred; nobody was frog-marched off the train at gunpoint, though a small gold and cream Spitz did cause a bit of a stir. The dog had passed the journey in a biddable manner, for the most part panting gently on the lap of a young woman or snoozing at her feet. When the guards barged into the compartment it skittered between their legs, leapt through an open window, landed on the glittering tracks with a sharp bark of surprise and took off. Its owner was a crinkle-haired blonde with luscious cherry-red lips and until the dog made its bid for freedom, the guards had been taking their own sweet time on her papers.

Hampered by bulky overcoats, the guards were diverting to watch as they chased, apprehended and eventually returned the nifty runaway to the young woman's arms but the dog's antics created further, unwelcome delay. It was close to Christmas; there was a war on and the vast majority of the passengers, whatever their religious or political affiliations, were keen to reach their destination as soon as possible. Not so the great thinker and authority on the relative nature of time, who was more than content with a delay; there were many reasons why arriving at his destination might prove as troublesome as failing to arrive.

Perhaps as he stoops to sniff the flowers, the boy's father pricks his finger on a thorn. Briar Rose, as everybody knows, pricked her finger on a spindle and then slept for a hundred

years, hidden behind a hedge of thorns. For the boy, his
father's ideas can be as impenetrable and entangled as a hedge
of thorns.

Stories. Once upon a time, when they were all together,
his father promised him and his brother a story and then,
caught up in some thought experiment about the laws of
the universe, he forgot about his promise, and the story; he
even forgot to come down from his study and join his family
for a supper of broth and bread. The boy could describe the
steaming bowls as they stood on the table that evening. He
could describe his father's palpable absence, the tenor of his
brother's cough, the knot in his mother's brow and the dark
hank of hair which fell into her eyes as she lowered them, in
stormy silence, to her food.

But that time is past and the boy considers himself too old
for stories. When he's poorly, which is much of the time, his
younger brother likes them and when their mother has a mind
for it, she will tell a Serbian story about Vodenjak, the water
sprite who steals souls. Vodenjak is green, frog-faced, covered
in slime and lurks under stones. On occasions when he favours
dry land, Vodenjak, like their absent father, smokes a pipe and
plays the violin.

The glint-eyed flower woman, with her craggy cheekbones
and a sceptical tilt to her chin, has almost given up hope of a
sale when the unkempt rose-sniffer – whose face is somehow
familiar – straightens up suddenly, knocking the umbrella
askew. He searches his pockets for his wallet until, wonder of
wonders, he locates it, and cheerfully hands over payment for
a dozen butter-yellow roses. He is pleased with his purchase,
pleased with himself for remembering that women like to be
given flowers. And pleased that he remembered his wallet.

Satisfied that, in this respect at least, he has done what is required of him, he turns his attention to the traders assembled on the vegetable bridge, engaged in the elastic give and take of commerce. There is more choice of food on the stalls than in Berlin and more refugees as well, offering handicrafts and family heirlooms for sale. He is taken with how each stallholder has fashioned a small cosmos from tables and wicker baskets, with wares deftly arranged in stacks and bundles and fans. How captivating the humdrum world can be with its humdrum concerns!

Midway across the bridge a twisted stick of a man saws away at a violin, his head and shoulders tossing and turning as if in thrall to a capricious wind. Unlike the citizens of Zürich, who barely break stride to part with their alms, the boy's father listens closely to several passages before placing a few *rappen* in the battered cap at the man's feet. To be sure, he thinks, the man plays badly but a badly played tune is better than no tune at all. Pleased with the shape of his own phrase, the boy's father decides that tonight, should he not play well for whatever company might assemble to celebrate his arrival, this will be his riposte. It is not his cleverest phrase but cleverness is not always required of him, at least where words are concerned. Too often, however, he finds himself pressed to pass judgement on topics and situations which do not concern or interest him, as well as those that do.

He looks forward to playing Mozart this evening – he has already decided that he will play only Mozart, looks forward to it more than anything. Music is not physics, yet for the life of him he would not be without it; indeed, music is part of physics. War is not physics either, and he would certainly be glad to be without war. He has said as much, in private and in public, and in no uncertain terms: war, he believes, will produce no victors, only the vanquished. War is not physics. Music is not physics. Market trading is not physics.

Now that he has made his purchase, which he knows full well is a peace offering – if a fragrant one – he would like a smoke. This poses a practical problem: even with the violin case lodged under an arm, the valise and the roses in the same hand, there remains the question of how he might hold a match to his pipe. He considers his options: to continue to his destination without a smoke; to light his pipe and attempt to continue walking and smoking, despite the awkwardness of such an arrangement and the likelihood that he will not, as result, fully appreciate his smoke; or to stop, make himself comfortable and yield to his desire.

He firmly believes that mankind should, in some matters at least, yield to its desires. If he did not believe this his boys would still have a father at home, and their mother a husband, though he is adamant that the time for such an arrangement has been and gone. As he is already late, and the church clock confirms this, a few minutes' pause will make a negligible difference in the grand scheme of things. As he is a devotee of the grand scheme of things, he deposits violin case, valise and flowers on the flat bridge wall, and fills his pipe. His mood lightens. His eyes twinkle with glee. After all, hasn't he proven that time has no independent existence?

What is in his valise? Sheet music, but of course. Bach and Mozart. A small jar of pickles. Small, modest gifts for the children. He disapproves of extravagance, materialism, greed. A bottle of calcium chloride, for the benefit of young teeth and bones: new research has indicated its beneficial effects. Notebooks – some already full of equations, others blank. A spare pen. A bottle of ink. A spare pipe. An extra tin of tobacco. A change of clothes. Shaving things. Basic toiletries, including a new toothbrush. A hairbrush he is unlikely to use.

The boy's father is everywhere. He's in the aromas of coffee
and tobacco which mingle and drift like rumours around café
and bierhalle doorways. He is in the newsstand headlines.
Sometimes there's a photograph of his soft, broad face caught
in an expression of wry congeniality beneath a mushroom of
hair. He's in the clatter of dray wheels, the snuffle and clop of
the droop-headed horses, in the tring-tring of trams swinging
onto Bahnhofstrasse, the klaxons of motor cars proclaiming
their arrival: *Here I am, here I am!* But when is this ever true of
his father?

His father is nowhere to be found in the dark days that
accompany his mother's increasingly contrary humours. Like
a restless revenant she paces to and fro, embarking on one
task then finding herself unable to complete it, starting on
something else then breaking off, muttering irritably until even
the walls quake in dismay. Or else, deep in the doldrums of
melancholy, she glares at the wall all day, insensible to pleading
and protestation, and the house takes on the funk of standing
water. Fires are rarely lit. Food is rarely cooked. The boys
learn to fend for themselves.

His father is everywhere: in the leaden ripples of the river,
in leafless branches creaking under the weight of snow, in
the lake's moody blue eye. The world says that his father has
his head in the clouds – which today are downy pillows of
cumulus and wispy mares' tails of cirrus – but that's not right:
his father has his head – and his sights – beyond the clouds,
beyond the farthest reaches of the sky, on something so tricky
to contemplate and articulate that it needs years of thinking
and screeds of workings out. And which, even after so much
time and effort, may never amount to more than an interesting

hypothesis. Rarely does he have his sights on his boys – the sturdy, surly one and the frail, sweet-natured one – or on their volatile, distraught mother.

In a tin box beneath his bed, the boy keeps every letter his father has written to him. His father is everywhere in the letters. He's in the smooth cream envelopes, with their Reichspost stamps depicting a steely Germania, in imperial crown and breastplate, olive branch in one hand, sword in the other. He's in the fuzzy black Berlin postmark, in the clean folds of the notepaper, in the small but fine hand, in the evenly spaced, perfectly formed letters, in the faint whiff of ink.

The boy has read the letters many times. He prefers to read them alone, in a secluded corner of the house. Though he knows their contents off by heart he needs to see the words on the page. When his father was writing to him, surely he must have been wondering what his son was doing at that very moment? And surely, while he sealed the envelope and walked to the post box, he would have continued to keep his son in mind, at least until he dispatched the letter and returned to his study to once more think about his big ideas? But why must his father remain in Berlin, why must he raise money for poor artists when he could be in Zürich with his own children?

His father is not in the crunch of snow as the boy throws himself on his sledge and careers down the slope in wild zigzags. *No other place is as nice for boys as Zürich, and so healthy,* his father wrote, at the beginning of the year. The boy's playmates do not tease him about the absence of his father; some of their own fathers are away from home, defending the Swiss borders. They are more impressed by who can be first down the hill. Rarely do these boys, all elbows and knees and ruddy cheeks, waste time on talk about absent fathers or distraught mothers. Rarely do they waste time on any kind of talk.

In his dreams his father is side by side with his son: hiking
in the mountains, walking and talking, in all weathers, all
seasons. They sing together, loud as you like, and clap each
time an echo greets them. They have such lightness of being
that they seem to walk above the surface of the ground. They
crane their necks to watch eagles circle slowly overhead or
to marvel at the daylight moon. Walking and talking, his father
presents him with problems and riddles – which in dreams the
boy can solve in a trice – and urges him to persevere with the
piano. Music, his father declares, is a kind of heaven and may
be the only heaven there is. And if the boy asks, as in dreams
he always does, when they will all be together once more, his
father vanishes.

Still perched on the wall of the bridge, the boy's father is
savouring his pipe when two squat matrons approach, in
large hats and fine fox furs, and bid him *guten Tag*. He has no
recollection of previously making the acquaintance of these
women, who are clearly not streetwalkers, and is temporarily
baffled by their forwardness. Then he remembers that few
people are in the habit of having their picture in a newspaper.
Briefly he wonders whether it would be possible to predict,
with an acceptable level of accuracy, the percentage of the
world's population who might have their picture in any
newspaper on any given day but deems the question not
worthy of his consideration. Surely, however, he will not
now be obliged to acknowledge greetings from multifarious
strangers? How much bowing and handshaking might this
entail!

His beautiful idea has become a beautiful theory and it
matters little at this point whether five or five thousand

understand it; what matters is that it is correct and even though he cannot yet foresee the ways in which it will irrevocably alter the cosmos, and humanity's conception of it, he continues to feel elated. And exhausted. He knocks the dottle from his pipe, picks up his violin case, valise and the flowers, and trudges onwards towards his destination: his family.

Would he have been permitted to cross the border? Were there really roses in the market in December, with thorns which might prick a careless finger? Or were there only scentless, poisonous, thornless Christmas roses, which don't at all fit with Briar Rose, her long sleep and her hedge of thorns? Did the flower seller and fox-furred ladies really recognise a stranger from a photograph in the newspaper? Would he ever arrive?

On winter mornings, when the boy walks to school in the dark, muffled up against the cold, his father is not beside him. Nor is he at the dinner table at midday, eating absently, anxious to finish his food and return to his thinking. When he struggles with his sums, his father is not there to help though his mother, when she is not marooned in despondency, is more than able to assist him. His father is in a place with no name, no dimensions, a place where time does not follow the tick of a clock, in a topsy-turvy place with few recognisable features, where everything is puzzling, unpredictable, a place which can barely be put into words.

To the faint strains of carol-singing the boy drags his sledge home, stows it in the shed, removes his boots and goes inside. The stove is lit, the kitchen is cosy and comforting, aromas of butter and nutmeg, cinnamon and sugar waft around. His mother, with his brother's help, is baking a cake. She doesn't smile but neither does she scold him for the wet footprints his socks leave on the kitchen floor. Instead of his father seated at the kitchen table, puffing on his pipe, is a letter, unopened, in a familiar but distant hand.

Malinger

Stella hated tears. Especially in the consulting room. At the tail
end of a long winter, being exposed to sniffs and snivels and
associated forms of mucoid expectoration was unavoidable;
she kept her distance and carried on. Lacrimal fluid was
another matter, the male variety in particular. Female tears
could usually be stanched by a plentiful supply of tissues and
maintaining deep eye contact for longer than she really had
time for. Male tears were rarer, trickier, and she wasn't sure
what was worse: the soundless ooze of an old boy's epiphora,
or the strangulated sobs of a forty-something, able-bodied
man, like the one who stared past her with such intensity
that she turned to see what had transfixed him. She could see
nothing but the overlapping slats of a beige venetian blind.

All the consulting rooms had blinds which remained closed
– for patient confidentiality – though it was doubtful that the
low, red-brick block drew much attention from passers-by.

Just around the corner, on the main street, were many more
alluring sights: animated knots of humanity glimpsed through
the windows of coffee shops; a greengrocer's display of
plump, perfectly formed fruit; buckets of scented blooms at
the florist's door; gift-shop windows decked out to simulate
treasure troves.

Of more interest to Stella was the public park where she
might occasionally snatch a brisk, head-flossing walk ahead
of afternoon surgery. That day she'd had no such luck. Her
lunch break was given over to arranging an ambulance for
old Mr Gunn, who had tumbled into the waiting room like a
bedraggled pigeon, clawing at his chest in a dumbshow of fear
and pain. He was in the early stages of a coronary. Time was
of the essence. His own GP, Jocky Craven, was taken up with
another possible emergency, which turned out to be a false
alarm, so she stepped in.

Why didn't he call an ambulance? Craven asked, once the
patient was on his way to A&E in the capable hands of a pair of
breezy paramedics.

Didn't want to make a nuisance of himself.

Gimme strength, said Craven. If he'd collapsed on the way
here he'd have made a damn sight more nuisance of himself.

Stella was running late. Very late. Doors were being closed,
keys turned in locks. Footsteps padded down the carpeted
corridor. Farewells floated through the sliding glass doors
which separated the consulting suite from the waiting room.

You're your own worst enemy, Craven said, sweeping out
of the building at six on the dot, followed closely by Mo, the
bossy, brassy receptionist, who reminded her, as if by then she
still didn't know the drill, to check the burglar alarm when she
locked up. As ever, Mo couldn't stay a moment longer; she

was not contracted beyond six, had responsibilities outwith the workplace. She wasn't the only one.

Stella pulled up the patient notes on screen and slid a box of tissues across the table.

Sorry for the wait. What seems to be the trouble, Mr Strang?

Rob, he sobbed. It's Rob! I was – sob – here last week.

Just a sec. The computer is sluggish today.

The computer was always sluggish.

Ah yes, she said. So you were. Insomnia. Any improvement? No.

She switched on the overhead light and the patient sprang into startling relief. His look had more than a touch of Jean-Luc Godard's New Wave: charcoal suit, black polo-neck and Chelsea boots, which might have been retro-cool had the suit not looked slept-in, the jersey not been flecked with lint and the boots crying out for a polish. His chin was stubbled, his floppy hair awry and there was more than a whiff of smoke and booze about him. At least it was the end of the day; the cleaners would air the room before the start of morning surgery.

That's better! she said brightly. Can't be sitting in the dark, though there is a lot of it about at this time of year.

I – sob – prefer the dark.

Well, yes, I'm a bit of a night owl myself but we all need light: daylight in particular.

I don't – sob – have SAD.

Seasonal affective disorder is more widespread than people imagine. And lightbox therapy can be surprisingly effective –

I don't – sob – need a SAD lamp! What's wrong with me is not – sob – season-specific. It's incessant.

Mr Strang – Rob – blew his nose noisily.

I can't – sniff – do this – sniff – anymore!

Stella offered a brisk smile. Was sniffing progress? She must focus on making progress.

Another door closed. More footsteps in the corridor. She was due to meet the gang after work. Food followed by a film. It was likely she'd have to miss the food and she'd already missed lunch. Wine on an empty stomach was a bad idea. She could bolt down her lunchtime sandwich though by now it would be limp and soggy from having spent ten hours in the staff fridge. She could grab a slice of pizza from a takeaway, or something less likely to make a mess. If she didn't want to abstain from wine – which, tonight, she really didn't – or find herself wracked with cramps after a couple of sips of white, she would have to eat *something*.

Once more, the sliding doors whooshed and clunked.

It was against regulations to work on without another staff member in the building but, rather than endure Mo heavy-footing it down the corridor, tutting and sighing, Stella was prepared to take her chances: the surgery had a direct line to the police station and the neighbourhood watch was nothing if not zealous.

So, Mr Strang – Rob – what is it you think you can't do anymore?

I don't *think* I can't, I *know* I can't!

Okay, so could you give me an idea of what you *know* you can't do?

Splitting hairs took up time she really couldn't spare but the patient seemed to require some pacification.

Any of it. I can't do *any* of it any more.

Now that doesn't sound good.

Stella suppressed a yawn. And a sigh. It was the time of day when her blood sugar as well as enthusiasm for her vocation dipped. Manifestations of existential angst were best dealt with earlier in the day. She scanned the symptoms the patient had previously presented to her: anxiety, low mood, insomnia, hyper-ventilation, heart palpitations, joint pain, loss of appetite, headaches, tinnitus, stomach cramps, exhaustion, lack of concentration. Stress. All too real, all too familiar. It was some small consolation that the patient had also consulted Craven recently about loss of libido and a rash in the groin area – but why hadn't he taken his string of stress-related ailments to the GP he was registered with, rather than to her?

Over the last few months, she'd run blood and urine tests. When he fretted about having some kind of tumour, she'd arranged X-rays, ultrasound and MRI scans. When nothing untoward showed up, he became anxious that the scans were inadequate, or the scanners faulty. She'd prescribed various medications, all of which he insisted caused adverse reactions or induced new symptoms. She'd suggested drug-free treatment, online self-help courses in stress reduction, which he claimed to have tried, to no avail. She'd written him sick line after sick line. Was he at it? Was he a hypochondriac, a malingerer? It was common enough for pressure to be put on junior doctors to supply unwarranted sick lines but did he really think that one of the most senior doctors in the practice was a soft touch?

Stella hated being spun a line. Especially by youngish, good-looking patients, with good jobs and good prospects. Of course, she couldn't be certain he was fabricating. It was human nature to embellish the truth but anybody could find a list of symptoms on the web and, in a ten-minute or even a twenty-minute appointment, how deeply could any doctor dig? Though he was more crumpled and dishevelled than she remembered, he didn't look *unwell*. His skin had a healthy glow, his spaniel eyes were clear, if pink-rimmed from weeping and, despite his avowed desperation, there was nothing of the defeated slump in his posture. On the contrary, he was straight-backed, gripping splayed knees with slender, smooth-skinned hands that had seen little manual labour.

She ran through a series of standard lifestyle questions on exercise, relaxation, diet, alcohol consumption – where most patient lying took place. His bored tone and clipped responses made it clear that he considered himself above such mundanities.

Could you maybe try, Mr Strang – Rob – to specify aspects of work you are finding particularly difficult?

All of it. Everything. The people, the place, the conditions, the atmosphere, the smell of the place gets to me. Even when I'm not in the building – when I'm at home, out with friends, when I'm falling asleep, *trying* to fall asleep, when I am, *eventually*, asleep, as soon as I wake up, before I'm barely conscious – it gets to me. It's all I think about, all I talk about. Not that anybody wants to hear.

There is no denying the adverse effects of work-related stress. How long have you been in your present employment?

Too long. Fifteen years. Fifteen years of being overworked and underappreciated.

Stella flung him the most fleeting of smiles. She had close on thirty years of being overworked. And if you include all the weekends on call, as Craven liked to remind her, that's another four years not accounted for. Four years! As for being underappreciated, you didn't really go into medicine to be appreciated, did you?

You're a teacher – is that correct?

Lecturer. Film Studies.

Nice.

It's not. At all. You have no idea.

Perhaps it wasn't the best choice of word but how hard could it be to watch a stack of films, form some opinions and be paid for the privilege? She loved everything about the cinema: the ubiquitous, ingrained smell of popcorn; the sweet and salty dark of the hushed auditorium; the swirl and ripple of the gilded curtains as they slid silently apart; the sense of being released from the relentless plod of time and the need to corral it into appointment-sized blocks.

Netflix was cheaper and more convenient than a trip to the cinema but had none of the magic of the big screen. And being able to pause and resume play at will somehow accentuated flaws in a storyline, cracks in character construction, laid bare contrivances and technical tricks. It was harder to be drawn in, to suspend disbelief, to ignore everyday demands, especially since Mick had become so much more dependent on her. It wasn't his fault that his concentration was shot after an hour or so, that he could no longer follow a complex plot, or needed, frequently, to be helped to the loo.

But don't you still love films?

Rob Strang sighed.

I no longer watch films for pleasure. I watch them because it's part of my job. Do you have to like people to tend to the sick? Besides, I don't teach film *appreciation*. Film *studies* takes a more theoretical – and increasingly philosophical approach. The focus is not whether a film is *enjoyable* but what it tells us about the societal structures within which it operates. If you ask the wrong questions – as I expect you know, Doctor – you are likely to get the wrong answers. Everybody knows that film is illusion, deception. Every angle, every shot, every word, every note of music exists to manipulate the viewer. When we imagine we see people walking and talking, we are not only watching an actor playing a part, we are fooled by the medium itself into believing that we see *motion*. Film studies asks whether film presents an imitation of reality or its own, different *reality*.

The sobs had dried up, the crack in his voice vanished and the tone had perked up considerably, as if Rob Strang had begun to address a roomful of rapt students.

Have you thought about a career change?

Don't make me laugh. I'm so very fortunate to be in gainful employment in such an illustrious institution. I really should go down on all fours to show my appreciation but the fact is I can't eat, I can't sleep, I can't concentrate. I can't do what I'm paid for. Not properly. Not the most important parts.

Which are?

Well, teaching, it goes without saying, which has to be squeezed into whatever space is left after information logging has eaten up the lion's share of my time and energy. But first and foremost is research. And forget the personal career development side, effective teaching is based on research.

Don't people in your position have sabbatical leave for that?

Some. Every so often. A sabbatical is supposed to be *supplementary to ongoing research*. Not the only time you can get around to doing any.

Ah. And what do you think might make things easier?

Not having to put up with all the bullshit, day in, day out. Not being badgered into producing endless reports. These people – middle managers, admin officers, website developers, data processors – don't, can't, or won't appreciate the abstract and essentially unquantifiable nature of the beast. How do you measure the genesis and development of an idea? How would you express the process on a spread sheet?

I have no idea, said Stella, making no disguise of glancing at the wall clock.

You don't, said Rob Strang. You can't. And yet these corporate cogs not only expect me to log my every move, they demand it, as if I'm some layabout who spends his days rearranging his bookshelves. Or a dolt who can't follow instructions. I'm not a layabout, nor a dolt. Nor am I a technophobe. Nor do I have time to spend a morning, afternoon or, God forbid, a *full day* becoming acquainted with another method of recording information. How many means and meridians, percentile points and averages does any teacher, or student, need? How many graphs and pie-charts?

Few people enjoy admin, said Stella, but there's no getting away from it. In the medical profession we –

I work hard! I want to be good at my job, I *need* to be good at my job but demands for some needless report or other drop into my inbox on a more or less daily basis – I'm not prone to exaggeration, doctor – and make it impossible to *think*. I am *expected* to think. I am *paid* to think yet everything seems to conspire to *prevent me from thinking*. By the time I get through a day of bureaucratic bullshit, I'm fit for nothing. But if I don't do the research, if I don't publish my findings, I lose credibility in my field. And if I lose credibility, the programme won't make enough profit – academia is a business and a cutthroat one at that – and sooner or later I will be out of a job. All because the powers that be *prevent* me from doing my job properly, the job I signed up for. Do you see the problem, doctor? The horse must come before the cart. The horse must come before the cart!

Once more Stella proffered the box of tissues but he waved them away.

No thanks. My crying jag is over.

So, what do you think would help? she asked. As if she didn't know.

She placed the box of tissues beside the desk tidy with its sheaf of ballpoint pens, freebies emblazoned with the logos of drug companies. These days she was rarely called upon to hand-write anything more than her signature on a printed prescription or sick line. Jocky Craven, whose writing implement of choice was his Montblanc Meisterstück, had been keeping a diary since his days as a houseman. He allotted a portion of each lunchbreak to blackening pages of one of his many Moleskines but kept them all guessing as to its contents. Stella didn't want to write a diary. She wanted the time to contemplate writing a diary.

It had been Stella's turn to choose the film. Her taste tended towards gritty, hard-hitting realism and tonight's feature was likely to be no exception. Set in present-day Norway and Afghanistan, the story revolved around the plight of an adolescent refugee caught up in organised crime. She anticipated some grumbles about the lack of premium placed on entertainment value. And the effort involved in having to read the subtitles. But wasn't the point of a film group to broaden horizons?

Over the years they'd had pleasant and unpleasant surprises, challenges to which only some had risen. Feathers had been ruffled. Boredom, bewilderment, disgust, hilarity had been voiced. There had been serious and not so serious differences of opinion. Fallings out and fallings off. Numbers had dwindled to half-a-dozen stalwarts, all of whom had become a tad predictable in their choices.

Not that the film mattered all that much. The post-mortem on what they'd seen tended to be brief, with conversation

segueing into a good old moanfest about work, the state of the
world, men. Over the past year, Stella had become less vocal
on the man-bashing front. Mick's condition had deteriorated
yet his graciousness in the face of suffering and indignity
remained; venting any gripes felt mean, disloyal. Besides,
people assumed that, given her line of work, she would have
expert coping strategies, which wasn't the case at all. And
knowing what to expect from Mick's continuing decline didn't
help at all. But a monthly night out with the film group could
remind her that there was more to life than illness.

Well? said Rob. Are you going to sign me off?

Taking a long spell off work, Mr – Rob, can create its own
problems. It might be better to sign you off on a weekly basis
and keep the situation under review.

That's no good. It will only add more stress. Can't you see
that?

The longer you're off, the harder it can be to go back.

I'll take a chance on that.

Stella was light-headed from hunger, from missing lunch
on account of Mr Gunn and his incipient coronary, Mr Gunn,
who wouldn't have wished anybody in the practice to address
him as *Alan*, although Mo got away with calling him *you old
rogue* when he forgot to bring along a urine sample. Alan Gunn
was another of Craven's patients who had taken to making
appointments with her, though only for complaints above the
waist or below the knee. Anything pertaining to his *nether parts*
he took to Craven. It wasn't a sick line he was after; he'd been
retired for years. So what was it – a gentler touch, a bit more
sympathy than Jocky had to spare?

Think yourself lucky, my dear, said Craven, as the
paramedics had wheeled Mr Gunn, soft and grey as putty,
down the path to the waiting ambulance. You have the man's

heart and mind. I'm stuck with his prostate, his piles and his penis.

She had intended to call the hospital mid-afternoon and check on Mr Gunn but no suitable window of time had materialised. Mo, in imperious mode, had plagued her with no end of piddling queries about repeat prescriptions and lab results, and the computer had been refusing, resolutely, to play ball. Her last appointment of the day had begun very late and then spilled well over the standard appointment time. The gang would already be ensconced in their favourite bistro, blethering at full tilt, as if they hadn't seen each other in years. One of the young, cute waiters would have poured each of them a glass of Prosecco and they would have gone ahead and ordered food because they knew how rubbish she was at time-keeping.

She checked that she had completed all the relevant boxes, double-checked the dates, printed out the form, added her signature with a stubby pink pen advertising a gel for dry eye. She slipped the sick line into an envelope, passed it to Rob Strang then stood up.

If there is any change – improvement or deterioration – you should contact Dr Craven in the first instance.

If you say so.

Stella escorted Rob Strang down the corridor and through the first sliding door. She waited as he made his way, rather more slowly than she would have liked, across the deserted waiting room and through the second sliding door which led to the street door, then returned to her consulting room. It had been dark when she arrived; it would be dark by the time she left. Before she shut down the computer and locked up, she checked with the hospital on Mr Gunn; she hoped his condition would be stable.

Arachne & Celeste

The spider is very black and shiny. It is a few inches away from
the bed, which formerly belonged to Lady Dark, and in which
Celeste will sleep for a full cycle of the moon. Some deep and
muddy taboo prevents her from harming even this one, in spite
of the fact that the country she is visiting hosts some of the
deadliest spiders in the world. She tries to trap her roommate
under a toothmug so she can release it into the night but
the spider senses the bell jar descend and scoots behind the
radiator. By the time she has returned to bed, the spider is
back where it was. Celeste looks at it, not too closely but in
a searching, concentrated way. It is inert, brightly black as a
mourning brooch which might have belonged to Lady Dark
and was, perhaps, a memento of a grand or great-grandmother
who, as a tough young pioneer built, bare-handed, the drystane
dyke around her modest patch of land, was reputed to have
a fondness for Black Heart Rum, black cockatoos, and equally

black arachnids.... Celeste continues to speculate on the Dark lineage as she turns off the bedside lamp. She hopes that the spider will be sympathetic to her bravery, her act of faith. The following night the spider joins her again, and every night thereafter, occupying the very same spot. Imagining it glittering through the night, Celeste sleeps unusually well. On the night before she has to leave the house – and the country – she glances once more at the wall. The spider is absent. She peers behind the radiator. Only some torn threads of cobweb remain. When she turns out the light she feels, for the first time in the Dark bed, a lacquered pang of loneliness.

Thirteen Minutes of Music

This is a story about two musicians. It could have been a story about a soloist, that lauded, lonely creature, the one and only one most pay their money to hear, no matter the quality of any supporting band. No, this is a story about a duo, classical as it happens. They could have been folkies, bluesers, jazzers, rockers, hip-hoppers and so on but I'm sticking with my original plan. I don't care to turn my pair into musicians who might appeal to a younger, cooler audience.

What I do care about is that this pair put in hours of practice every day. They are clean-cut, clean-living. Mostly. Nobody's perfect. For performances they favour traditional concert garb: black on black with, perhaps, a bit of sparkle to catch the light. Their hair is clean and neat unless they're of a mind to let their locks grow wild and tangled; not, you understand, to be hip, but as a nod to some wild and tangled virtuosi of the past. Go back a hundred years, two hundred, and this pair wouldn't look very different from how they look today.

How they looked yesterday is another matter. Last night. Late last night. Very. Long past the witching hour, when sensible classical musicians should be abed, in a nice hotel room if they are lucky, a not-so-nice boarding house room otherwise, instruments within arm's reach – unless they are pianists, harpists or timpanists – clothes for the following day's performance de-wrinkling in a wardrobe, on a rail, on the back of a door.

Our two musicians are young, very young, still in their late teens, though they have performed together in twenty-three countries, or twenty-eight, depending on how you define a country. But I've been vague. *Musician* is a very vague term. Anybody who can get a decent sound out of an instrument, any instrument, might be termed a musician. And I haven't even mentioned gender, appearance, background. OK, so boy and girl. The boy plays violin, the girl piano. For as long as they can remember, music has been their life and now, when they walk on stage, before a single note has been heard, they are rewarded with a warm wave of applause.

They are also rewarded with the freedom and privilege of international travel. They shop for shoes in Italy, sunglasses in Singapore, have jackets made to measure in Hong Kong or Hanoi. The boy's violin was made thousands of miles from his birthplace and has its own illustrious lineage. It is rarely feasible for the girl to travel with her piano but if the instrument provided does not come up to scratch and she has to have words with a venue manager, she can count on the boy to take her side.

The boy and girl are related. I didn't want them to be siblings or first cousins. Second cousins, perhaps, so that, if *chemistry* were in the air, they might embark on a torrid affair with no more tongues than usual wagging; they might go forth and multiply, free from qualms about offspring having too few or too many digits. Not that any such entanglement is a pressing consideration.

Much has been invested in this duo. Not long after each mastered the art of directing a mush-laden spoon into an open mouth, a parent or relation noticed that when one or other had eaten their fill, they began to beat spoon against bowl in a distinctly rhythmic manner, and to hum along tunefully to the beat – they were musical!

The faintly disconcerting discovery was shared with other family members, who paused in their soup-stirring, tea-tasting, beer-swigging, their channel-surfing, texting, tweeting and Googling to consider the implications. I could have chosen a poor, close-knit, virtuous family, a corrupt but solvent family, a distant but scandalously wealthy family. I could have chosen a cool, controlling household, a warm, free-wheeling or chaotic, emotionally volatile household but whoever was directly responsible for the upbringing of the musical kiddiewink realised, with a heady fizz of pride and awe, that the child must have an instrument and learn to play it. Well.

The child, who fortunately is endowed with a photogenic countenance and bodily charm, must practise while siblings and schoolmates run free in sun or snow, watch TV or feast their ears on the latest chart-toppers, must rise early while others slumber on, must forego activities which might damage priceless hands, must at all times be mindful of the special gift from God or genetics.

And make the most of it, for everybody's sake: for the child, whether or not it is of any personal interest; for the parents, who hope to benefit in incalculable if mostly financial ways; for dignitaries in their home town, state, nation who, should anything come of a family's investment and a childhood given over to mastering an instrument, would jump at the chance to claim the achievement as their own and exploit to the full any reflected glory.

Not that our young musicians constantly keep in mind this imposed role of ambassador, mascot, shining example, local resource, especially now that they have reached the dizzy heights which their parents hoped, prayed, saved and paid through the nose for them to reach. Now that they are ensconced in the starry firmament of success by virtue of their gift and their hard work, there are times when our duo really couldn't care less whether or not the mayor, the minister of culture or the local TV anchorperson is satisfied.

But let me backtrack to where I left off. No, a little further back. The boy and girl were waiting in the departure lounge of the main airport of their homeland. They had checked in their baggage and gone through security, where the boy's violin case was thoroughly searched in case it contained unaccountable wads of cash, illegal substances, firearms or explosives. One of the security officers, a music lover, recognised the duo and apologised profusely for the inconvenience.

It's okay, said the boy. I'm used to it.

Musicians are not a special case, said the girl.

They were in the middle of their third game of Chinese chequers. The boy preferred chess but the girl had little patience with its slow, strategic moves. Chequers was a compromise. And airport chequers had become a tradition. Both played to win. The girl was two games ahead and the boy was becoming bored – he was always more enthusiastic when he was in the lead – when an announcement crackled across the tannoy that all flights were delayed.

The arrivals and departures boards shuffled and flashed. The TV screen, which had previously been featuring the world fencing championships, now showed blurry, disjointed footage of the city centre. A red news ticker ran on a loop along the bottom: Armed Rebels Take Over Conservatoire – break into packed concert hall – doors barricaded – armed with grenades and sub-machine guns – hostages taken – security forces not ruling out possibility of explosive vests – Armed Rebels Take Over –

The boy and girl stared numbly at the screen. They had been invited to visit the conservatoire, *their* conservatoire, to take part in that very concert. Only a few weeks back one of their former teachers had invited them, in fact come close to begging them, to give a short recital, as guests of honour. It would be wonderful if they could also stay to hear some of the up-and-coming talent. The duo declined the invitation. It would have been a rush to fit in even a fleeting appearance before their flight and rushing wasn't good for people who had to perform at a major international festival the following day. Calm was required: relaxation, preparation.

The girl had wanted to squeeze in an appearance but the boy had been adamant about turning it down. They had argued, he declaring it was too much trouble, she insisting they owed a debt to the institution which had nurtured them until public recognition brought personal mentors, the best rehearsal rooms and a string of high-profile bookings. They had argued but not seriously. The conservatoire would invite them another time. As it was, it invited them rather too often.

On the screen, a shaky lens panned over the inside of the concert hall. Transfixed, the boy and girl clutched each other. Friends, teachers, rivals – many of the defining relationships of their lives were bound up in that baroque, high-ceilinged hall with its gilt, cobwebbed cherubs, its flaking coral and turquoise walls, its electric chandeliers, the pervading odour of uncured sheepskin and damp plaster. Friends, teachers, rivals were being shoved about and shouted at by ragged rebels who, as well as making more significant demands, wanted uniforms – with brass buttons! – so they'd be recognised as a proper army.

In close-up, a young woman was shown dismantling and packing away her flute, at gunpoint. Then the screen went blank. In the departure lounge the delayed passengers howled, wailed, paced around, continued to stare at the blank screen. Nobody could get a signal on their phone. A few attempted to go back through the security barriers but the guards had their guns up: nobody was going anywhere. Yet. Further information would be forthcoming. In the meantime, everybody should keep calm and obey instructions.

The girl shrank into herself. The boy stared out into the dark. His thoughts made him flush with shame. Alongside worrying about who was caught up in the siege – and it was as well that the images were too blurry to identify anybody – the question of whether they would get to play the Debussy the following day wouldn't go away. The concert was to have been their first performance of Debussy's last major composition. Those thirteen minutes of music had stretched them, pushed them to the limit. Both loved the piece. How many hours had they practised it? To think about playing the Debussy was wrong.

A shabby, shambling man, arms raised to the floodlit ceiling, approached.

Play something, fiddler boy. Any fucking thing.

For a long, dark moment the boy eyed the man then, yes, he took out his violin, checked the tuning quickly, quietly, then

raised it to his chin and began to play. And yes, the trapped
passengers turned their ears to the source of the sound. The
sound was beautiful and solemn. They listened, and in their
mind's eye saw all the twists and turns of a life, the halting
steps, the reckless leaps in the dark, the grey mist and the red,
the pull of spirit and blood.

The boy played and the girl tapped a ghostly
accompaniment on the stained, gritty plush of the seat. They
didn't entertain everybody in the airport until take-off. They
played a half-audible, half silent version of Debussy's last Violin
Sonata then sat mute for hours. As did most of the other
passengers. Sometimes people closed their eyes, sometimes
they looked out to where the grounded planes stood, in
the dark spaces between the landing lights. Every so often
somebody cracked and tried to storm the security barriers.
Two women and a man were hauled off by the guards.

Sometime after midnight, with the hostage situation still
unresolved, the plane took off. In the small hours, it arrived
at its destination. After a long wait for a taxi then a long drive
into the slumbering city, the boy and girl arrived at their
hotel. Their clothes were crumpled, hair wild and tangled.
They were about to climb the steps to the glass and chrome
revolving door when a lone, late-night reveller lolloped across
the deserted street, wrenched the violin case from the boy,
slammed it against the railings then lurched off, rawboned,
inebriated, coatless despite the cold. His guffaws hung in the
still air. Dawn was breaking. The boy and girl were booked to
play at noon. They were so tired.

Smoke-Long Story

Zbig stands in the back lane beside bin bags gutted by a seagull
or a city fox, shields his cigarette against the gritty wind and
considers his choices:

go back inside after the smoke break and deck the money-
grabbing bastard boss who docked his wages for being late to
work –

go home to his wife, a local girl he might not have given a
second look but when the baby was on the way he wanted to
do the decent thing and now his bastard boss has docked his
wages –

go round to the corner shop, buy a flat quarter bottle, or
maybe a half – either would slip into his pocket – do the
rounds of the park bench boozers, stop when he hears folk
speaking his own language –

go back inside wearing the chiselled smile of a man who has no alternative –

go back inside and trash the place –

go back inside, slip on the boss's leather jacket with the fur collar and leave like a weasel –

phone Tad, the bright-eyed dolt who followed him here, who'd swallowed the shit he'd fed him about grass is greener and life is sweeter – check whether the doctor has seen to his head wound and if the kid's not out cold let rip about his bastard boss who can't understand that a man has other things to think about than the lunchtime service –

dig loose change from his pockets, take a bus to the coast, fill his lungs with sea air, scoop up handfuls of damp sand, let the soggy grains slip through his fingers and add up how much more, for how much longer –

go to the skanky internet caf, check online for cheap flights home – right now the trees would be golden, the plums ripe, his mother standing with a full basket at the end of the narrow plot, squinting into the fat, autumn sun, the crackling sky loaded with thunder, the slow, sweet-voiced girl from high school, pouring beer and plum brandy in the village bar, laughing at jokes about the ones that got away and not caring about her bad teeth –

Zbig's smoke – and his break – are done. He lights up another.

Gorgon's Final Curtain

When he heard he'd been picked to go on the show, the first thing Gorgon did was take his motor for a spin, the souped-up, canary yellow hatchback with the personalised number plate: GORGO19. He was nineteen. His name was Gordon but that was boring so his mates called him Gorgon because he was a monster. They'd called him that for ages before they realised Gorgons were female and by then the name had stuck. He gunned up the dual carriageway which cut through the scheme like a jugular and was wide enough for the emergency services to make an entrance, though due to the industrial-sized speed bumps they had to restrain themselves more than they were in the habit of doing: countless vehicles had already impacted on the bumps at way over the limit and the burst bricks had morphed into tyre busters.

Gorgon knew the location of every misshapen or misaligned brick and could rev himself up to a speed which would more than merit a fine. In their quest for something meaningful to do with their weekdays, weeknights and weekends, he and his mates blasted up and down the dual carriageway: any day of the week, time of night, it was all the same. Work wasn't something that entered into the equation in a big way and when it did the reality was always pish: a couple of days chucking scaffolding around, rolling barrels off ramps, shoving a nozzle into the petrol tank of some other cunt's motor when they could be filling their own tanks with what they'd siphoned off some rich bitch up the town.

Gorgon's motor was his babe, his dreamboat, his pride and joy. When he read in some free paper that the fastest drivers favoured yellow cars well, red rag to a bull, he got Bogs to do him a cheap sprayjob. Bogs had casual work in a garage and managed to fit in a few homers on the side. The numbskull had missed a bit on the roof but the red stripe against the yellow looked like it might have been intentional. The custom number plate cost him but paid its way: Gorgon liked to be noticed, to make a statement.

As for the interior, he'd looked long and hard through the auto-fitters that trailed along the industrial drag otherwise known as Seafield. When he saw the fake fur zebra-striped seat covers (100% polyester, machine-washable) there was no competition. He got the dosh off his ma who was chuffed at him taking an interest in such a practical thing as upholstery, though his main aim was to turn the interior into a safari love shack, in the hope it would up his chances of pulling. When his nan saw the zebra covers, she trotted down to Poundsaver in her poodle boots and came back with a humungous pair of furry dice for him to dangle below his rear-view mirror. Gorgon gave her a kiss, a right smacker, on a cheek as wrinkled and green as a dodgy sultana.

Ye're a lovely laddie, she said. Yin o they days, ye'll make some lassie happy.

Yin o they days was about to become a reality.

Stopped at the lights, he opened the window and gave everyone in the vicinity the benefit of his heavy-duty bass. Gorgon liked to make a statement and now he'd been picked and given a date for the show, he was planning to make as big a statement as possible. It was official. From the thousands who'd sent in their details, he, Gordon Methill, was one of the chosen.

A group of females was stopped at the crossing and he'd have roared by them, sound system blasting their lugholes but the lights turned red and you couldn't really mow down a bunch of young mums with buggies, so he jammed on the brakes and slammed a hand against the steering wheel in time to the beat, while the whole sorry bunch of them trauchled across the carriageway. Trauchled and waddled. Lassies with bairns, wifies with bunches of Lidl bags. Built like sumos, the lot of them. The bairns – and they were all bruisers too – were girnin and greetin. Except for the wee Asian babby and its wee Asian mammy, in matching purple parkas which set off the bronzy sheen of their skin. Bogs had a motor exactly the same colour and Gorgon had to admit the colour had class, a sleek, untouchable class. The wee Asian mammy and babby followed the sumos across the road, eyeing him anxiously with wide, treacly eyes.

On the show there would be all sorts: blondes, redheads, brunettes, Asian birds, Chinese birds, Jamaican birds, posh birds with good skin and a natural tan, not a fake bake which was basically a sprayjob. A whole roomful of birds, dressed to kill, for him to impress, woo, do a number on. Things were looking up, looking up in such a big way he found himself

waving at the sumo mums and their brats, trying out the
wave he'd give when he walked on the set, the winning wave,
and the look that would make every bird on the show wet
her knickers. Or melt. Or whatever it was birds did in the
situation.

He'd have to practise. Walk the walk, talk the talk. Pick the
outfit – that was priority – then get the haircut. He dunted
the furry dice, made them dance about. He was on a roll. Bogs
and Lonnie would be sick with envy. Pure sick. They'd given
him grief about putting his name down for the show, making
out it was for losers but that was just the green-eyed monster
talking and they could go take a running jump. It was a win-win
situation. Near enough. The odds were stacked in favour of
the guy, very much in favour of the guy, of him, Gorgon!

The lights turned green and Gorgon drove through the
arse end of the scheme and made for the beach, which was
where he did his thinking – when he needed to think – and
there was no denying it, this needed the brain in gear. No
point in getting picked then blowing it. It did happen. But
rarely, very rarely. He wasn't going on the show because he
was a loser, no way, he just didn't fancy what was on offer
round his bit. Half the lassies his age already had bairns of their
own and the other half were dogs or slags or junkies who'd
got old before their time – he wanted a babe, deserved a babe:
he was fit, kept his motor in tip-top condition, was good to his
ma and his nan, Lynxed his oxters – what more could a lassie
want?

The beach was quiet. Only a few folk exercising their dogs, old
folks mostly who eked out their days with trips to the shops,
taking the dog for a walk, the box. Not that different from
his own routine – apart from the dogs – but he was a young

laddie, wouldn't be doing this shit forever, something better
would come along. And soon, by the looks of things, very
soon!

Some of the birds on the show had money as well as class,
and liked to let everybody know about it. If he made the right
choice he could be well sorted, get himself out of the dump
he called home. Smart thinking, Gorgon, smart thinking. A rich
bird, maybe even one a bit older, a wee bit older, he wasn't
about to get himself lumbered with some Antiques Roadshow
number, no way, but a mature bird, into the idea of a toyboy,
who'd be so chuffed to have a young laddie like him she
wouldn't bother that he didn't have a job and lived with his ma.
She'd have the dosh for the both of them and her own place
to get down to it. And wouldn't bother if he had a wee fling
when the fancy took him. With a younger, prettier bird, like.
And wouldn't kick up a stink if he had nights out and weekends
away with the lads because the bottom line was she'd be
grateful for what she could get. Aye.

The sky was grey as per usual, the sun as washed-out as
the moon, no heat off it. The beach was contaminated so you
couldn't eat the mussels or the crabs. It was stony and oily
with spillage from the rigs and the tideline was crusted with
litter and broken glass but if you ignored all that – and you had
to ignore it or you were sunk – it was an okay place to be: a
few mutts loping about and the waves making wee frills on the
shoreline.

He'd tell them on the show that he lived by the beach.
Always a plus, contaminated or no. Not exactly on the
doorstep but near enough if, like him, you had wheels. Easy-
peasy, Gorgon, you'll charm the birds off their perches, out
of their cages. He stood at the water's edge. The water was
smooth as a clean sheet. Silk sheets, man, a kingsize, no a

superkingsize bed, now that would be the business. A wave
rushed up and soaked his trainers right through to his socks.
Fuck.

When he told Bogs and Lonnie about being selected, they
pumped him full of vodka and talked as dirty as they could
manage until they ran out of obscenities and slumped on his
ma's sale of the century L-shaped settee, a slashed price, four
years' credit, pay-nothing-for-the-first-twelve-months deal that
took up the entire living room. Blootered to fuck they were.
Battered. Tanked. Gorgon paid no heed to their suggestions
for knock-em-dead lines. He had his own:

*I call ma motor the Scottish safari love nest. Bring the ootdoors
indoors. Bring the wildness inside.*

On the subject of what he should wear, well he had his
own ideas about that and spent hours communing with his
mirror, trying on everything he owned, and every expression
he could muster: hot and smouldering, wee boy lost, mean
and moody, party animal. Mostly he felt mean and moody
was the best option: treat em mean and keep em keen, that
was the ticket. His teeth let him down if he smiled too much
and anyway who wants to look like a pushover? Show your
sensitive side at the final countdown. If at all.

He couldn't find anything in his wardrobe which didn't
look shabby or chavvy in a way he didn't consider befitted the
occasion so his ma shelled out for a new jacket and shoes. He
didn't ask and she didn't say where the dosh came from. She'd
be owing somebody somewhere but her laddie would be on
the box so something sometime was bound to bounce back
her way. A pal, well a sort of pal, worked up the town in a hot
shave barber's that specialised in signature buzzcuts: any design
you wanted. As Gorgon liked to keep to a theme, he went for
zebra stripes: a centimetre of stubble, dyed black, against areas

of shaved white skull – well, to be honest, more of a gummy pink.

Way to go, said Bogs and Lonnie.

Have you got time tae grow it oot? said his ma.

It was too late for that. And too late to return the jacket, not that returning it was ever on the agenda. He loved it. Yellow like his motor, with a wee red lion rampant on the breast pocket, to show the world he was a Scot and proud of it. The shoes were red brogues, with curly tongues, to match the lion.

I like tae make a statement, he said to the gay guy in the clothes shop, who rolled his eyes like a fruit machine about to stop on lemons, then sucked his lips into the shape of a single cherry. Bogs stuck the shades on when Gorgon gave his mates a twirl. Lonnie just shook his head dead slow and banged on about taking along a spare jacket, for emergencies.

Whit if ye spill something on aw that yellae, likesay ketchup or broon sauce? Ye dinny want tae look like a twat, man. No on the box.

When he was sent to makeup he baulked at the very idea.

That's for lassies and poofs, he protested, but the makeup girl, who was just short of being a stunner even if she was wearing beat-up jeans and a baggy top, said everyone on the telly wore slap because of how the lights made your skin look funny, so he let her powder his nose with a big fluffy brush that tickled and made him sneeze. He was getting the hots for her but cooled down again when she started dabbing cover-stick on the pimples on his nose and chin and forehead, and plucked a bunch of rogue hairs from between his eyebrows. She was from Australia. Her name was Heather.

I like your accent, said Heather. Some people down here say they can't understand Scottish but I'm just dandy with it.

So ye should be, said Gorgon.

Scotland's a beautiful country. The Highlands, the lochs, the mountains. So grand and romantic.

It's no that bonny roon ma bit, said Gorgon. I'm in the Central Belt. Industrial, ken. Except there's nae fuckin industry nae mair. Sorry for swearin, ken.

But it's still your country. Still something to be proud of.

Aye, right enough, darlin.

He was getting the jitters, wanted to get on with it, get out on the set and meet the birds, the babes, he'd been waiting long enough for this moment, it was time to get the show on the road. Heather said there was usually a wait.

Time to change your mind. Or your outfit.

Who's gonny change their mind, who's gonny crap out?

You'd be surprised. And how many change their gear at the last moment. I'm sure you thought long and hard about what to wear and all but –

Too right, darlin. The jaikit's got the wow factor, no?

Sure, but the thing is mate – and I'm only trying to help – the yellow fights with the studio lights. Starts to kinda throb.

Fine wi me, darlin. Gie me some throbbin!

Everybody's going to notice the jacket more than they're going to notice you. And that would be a real shame. If you have anything else?

To shut Lonnie up, he'd brought along the charcoal number he'd worn for his uncle Tony's funeral but no way was he wearing that. You had to make a statement, to stand out from the crowd.

Course I have somethin else wi me, he said. But it's me who's gaun on the show and naebody's gonny cramp ma style. Nae offence n'that.

Gorgon's heart was pounding, his legs were numb as he

walked down the wide, shallow steps and on to the set. He
had to think through every movement. It was like his brain
and his body had a loose connection or something but then he
saw them, the array of birds lined up in a great glittering arc
across the stage, in sequins, velveteen, satin and lace, leather
and denim. Each was encased in a cage of lights like a bird of
paradise.

The noise was mental, a tsunami of shrieks and hollers as
he made his entrance, the boy who'd waved goodbye to his
ma that morning after a breakfast of strong tea, sausages and
fried bread, who'd showered in the tepid drip that was all the
council provided, the boy who'd given the finger to Bogs for
putting on the shades again as Gorgon took the bus up the
dual carriageway – no way was he paying the station parking
charge – who'd given the finger to Lonnie, tramping up to the
bookies and doing the slow headshake again, the fucker. He
wasn't even wearing the gear on the bus, of course not, he was
keeping it nice, in the sports bag.

And then he was on the train. It had cost the price of a pint
for the seat reservation and he was stuck beside a fat cow who
jabbered on her phone non-stop, letting the whole carriage
know about some half a million deal she'd clinched and how
solicitors deserved the weekend off like everybody else and
she was going to spend hers sailing, come hell or high water.
Gorgon had forgotten his phone, something was wrong with
the bootleg iPod so he had nothing to do the whole way down
but go over his moves and the knock-em-dead soundbites in
his head, when he could hear himself think.

He stops, as instructed, in front of each of the birdcages,
does his twirl and flashes his mean and moody look – and now
he's loving it, the swing of the jacket, the way the birds eyeball
him and only him, size him up and oh yeah, they like what they

see, they've all got big cheesy grins on their faces. He walks
down the line feeling like a king, an emperor, a god supping
his nectar, taking in the slinky curves, the bare shoulders,
cleavages deep as the Grand Canyon which he's never seen
and probably never will but who cares, these babes have grand
canyons of their own and legs up to their necks –

But before he's even opened his mouth, before he's done
more than walk past them, the birds are pressing their buttons
and curtains drop from the ceiling and cover up the cages. Half
of them are already out of the game. More than half. Before
he's even opened his mouth. And when he says,

I'm Gorgon fae Scotland. I call ma motor the Scottish safari
lovenest!

The curtains drop again until there's only two left. Two!
One's a giant, the other's half his height and twice as wide, and
the show host is saying it's time for his last shot.

Go for it, laddie, he says. Ye're still in wi a chaunce. The
show host's Scottish accent is crap.

And this is the point when he's expected to do his party
piece, but where's the party?

Come on, son, the host hisses in his ear, we've got a
schedule to keep.

Gorgon clears his throat and starts the song his nan sang
when he was wee:

Yew ur ma sunshine, ma only sunshine, Yew make me haaapae
when skies ur grey.

One curtain drops but he keeps going, his voice sounding
like the words are being pushed through a cheesegrater:

Yew'll never know dear, how much ah luuuve yew, Please don't
take ma sunshine –

The final curtain drops with a heavy, dead sound, and
the whole thing's over so fast he doesn't know what's hit

him though it feels like it must have been a truck at full belt because nothing is registering except the slick, smarmy show host with the no-colour, no-impact suit and the fake bake hugging him – a guy, a complete stranger hugging him for fucksake – clapping him on the back and ushering him towards the EXIT sign which is flashing and means it's over, it's all over and he has to leave.

But he's meant to leave with a date! A date with a babe! And he's dateless, babeless. Not one of them, not a single one of them stayed in the game. When the host asked why they'd turned him down, some of them poked their beaks out from behind the curtains of their cages and said they couldn't make out what he was saying. Said he didn't speak their language. And they were from all over the place, all over, and he had no trouble with understanding the shit they came out with. He could even pinpoint where most of them came from: Birmingham, Liverpool, Newcastle, London – *Saaf* London, Swansea, Belfast, Carlisle. Places he's never been.

On his way out of the building, Gorgon kicks up a stushie with the security guards who are in way too much of a hurry to get him off the premises and bundle him into a taxi bound for the station. The producer has sent down one of his poncey minions to press a bottle of whisky into his hands – he fucking hates whisky – and tell him what a great guy he is, all the production people agree, it was just the luck of the draw, the choice of females, something in the air, the water, the hard Southern water.

It's early morning, way too early when the train pulls into the Waverley. He'd head home but his ma does a morning cleaning job and wouldn't appreciate an even earlier rise than usual. He walks all the way down the hill from the station. Miles. The

shops are boarded up and the pubs won't be open for hours.
Since he got the motor he doesn't do a lot of walking but it's
okay. He kicks a few bollards, boots a pizza box, heads it. He
has the place to himself, apart from the gulls squabbling over
the remains of takeaways. Mine, they screech. Mine!

The sky is a pinky grey. The top of the oilrig wears a crown
of mist and the water is calm. Just a whisper as the tide creeps
up on the shore. The beach is cleaner than usual. Some folk
must have been roped in to a bit of community service but
give it a couple of days and it'll be back to its usual. Gorgon
stops at the water's edge, takes in deep lungfuls of salty air.
His red leather shoes sink into the sand. He runs a hand over
his head, feels the new stubble growing in, spoiling the zebra
stripes. He takes off the jacket, spreads it front side up on
the water so the wee lion rampant is cushioned on a bed of
yellow, watches as it drifts out on the tide and wonders how
the fuck how he's going to square it with his ma, his nan and
his mates.

Hairball

The house groaned, it growled, it roared, it sicked up a hairball of outlandish proportions, as if every cat which had ever sat on the doormat had added its own gruesome contribution; or every horsehair sofa which had ever served the living room, weary of all those arses shifting irritably, rubbing away plush, needlecord or leather upholstery, weary of having to endure generations of gripes and moans, of simmering resentment and blasts of blowtorch rage, had burst its buttons all at once and disgorged its stuffing. What relief, what joy to get it all out in the open, spit it onto the street. An eyesore for the neighbours to be sure. There would be letters of complaint, and threats to report the residents to the council if they didn't dispose of their festering domestic unrest with promptness and consideration. But inside the house, in the absence of the hairball, what calm has taken its place, what an expanse of space and light. The door is always open now. Step inside.

Young

It had been a miserable summer, weeks of damp gloom, the grass in the back green too sodden to cut, the shrubs and hardy perennials in the border rotting at the roots, but Mel couldn't care less about the weather or the state of the communal plot. Mid-afternoon, after another all-nighter in clubland, getting up to who knows what reckless, unhealthy and illegal activities, her daughter Bonnie was out for the count beneath a rancid duvet, amid the mingled stinks of booze, weed, takeaway food and adolescent hormones.

Electrical wires from phone charger, hair straighteners, blow-dryer and laptop trailed and tangled through a midden of dirty laundry. Squalor was one thing; a fire hazard was another. The hair straighteners had already scorched the carpet and the dressing table: nothing Mel said about safety in the home or the tragic life of burn victims had any more effect than spit on a conflagration. Nothing Mel said about anything had any effect.

Her daughter didn't want to hear her mother, see her mother, speak to her, share the same air. Mel was reduced to skulking around, an outcast in her own home.

Scott, Mel's husband, was off in rural France. His emails told of breathtaking bike rides to sleepy villages, of unbroken sunshine by day and dramatic thunderstorms by night, of jaunts to Paris: the art galleries, the boulevards, the *confit de canard,* the *coq au vin,* the *vin.* It was a working break of sorts and Mel would have been glad for him had Bonnie's simmering resentment not doubled on his departure. Had her mother pissed off as well, she could have had the run of the place and hosted any number of house parties.

Days went by with barely a word passing between mother and daughter. There was never the right time for meaningful conversation, for any kind of conversation at all. If it wasn't friends, it was *Friends,* or *Desperate Housewives,* or *Big Brother.* Bonnie had to go out, to do something on the computer, to phone a friend, dry her hair. Often the computer, phone, TV and hairdryer were all going at the same time, as if her aim were to max out her carbon footprint.

When the rain finally let up, Mel dragged the lawnmower from the dank, filthy shed. The grass was long and lush, bristling with dandelions and hard to mow but it was good to feel the sun on her face and focus on a simple goal. She was about to charge into the last swishing, uncut patch when a fat bird bobbed out from the weed-infested border and shuttled briskly across the newly cut, sweet-smelling grass. It was a gull chick, with downy speckled feathers. A very large gull chick.

Mel completed the mowing, returned the Flymo to its home amid broken chairs, bicycle wheels, skis – whose were the skis? – and other assorted crap which nobody ever saw fit to take to the dump. Then she stuffed the compost bin with grass cuttings. She didn't like the compost bin much. It seethed with the festering and decomposing. It generated its own heat and bustle. Just imagine falling into all that feverish activity.

The chick blinked, turned its back on her and crooed softly; its pillowy bulk quivered. It showed no sign of fear or any likelihood of shifting from the spot. Had it been injured, damaged a wing? She was bending to check its condition when a fierce screeching erupted overhead. Before she had time to locate the source of the racket, a pair of adult gulls whooshed past her ears so close that their wings skimmed her cheeks. Screeching all the while, the gulls rose up again, twisted in mid-air and launched a second synchronised assault. Shielding her face, Mel backed off from the chick and irritably took refuge indoors. It was the first fine day in weeks, for God's sakes, and she couldn't even enjoy being out of doors.

Gulls had only recently begun to nest in the city centre but they'd quickly made their mark, splattering walls and laundry pegged on clotheslines, fouling up house windows and car windscreens with viscous, corrosive slugs of yellow-green guano. They bawled to each other from chimney tops and swanked on the pavements with the insolent, proprietorial glare of occupying troops. They basked on sun-warmed bonnets of parked cars and harassed indigenous pigeons over anything edible.

The chick had plumped itself down on a sunny patch of grass and closed its smug little eyes. Mel kept the cat indoors though couldn't put any such restraints on her daughter, who surfaced late afternoon, slumped in front of *Friends* re-runs with the volume cranked up so high that canned laughter spilled into every corner of the flat. After gulping down an overflowing bowl of cereal, Bonnie spent the next couple of hours between the bathroom mirror and her bedroom mirror.

At dusk, without a civil or uncivil word, she traipsed out into the night – too much cleavage, too much leg, too much makeup – leaving a trail of damp towels, discarded clothes and blistering contempt.

Mel shed a few tears. They came easily these days. Her reservoir had filled to the limit and brimmed over at the least provocation. Though she was under orders not to enter Bonnie's room, she ventured in, glancing around anxiously, as if she expected something nasty to be lying in wait for her, a trap of some kind. But no, there was just the mess. She switched off all electrical appliances, removed pizza boxes and beer cans and made surreptitious inroads into the mountain of laundry.

As the washing machine sloshed into action, she attempted to get to grips with some paperwork – she'd promised Scott she'd attend to her tax return and some new forms from the Child Benefit office – but soon gave in to maternal brooding. The sky turned fuschia, purple, indigo. The chick was still on the grass, making aimless little forays this way and that. It couldn't fly; it didn't even seem to know it had wings.

Mel didn't like gulls but a chick was a chick and when night fell wouldn't it be picked off by some nocturnal predator? Surely a fox would rip it to bits, or one of the burly neighbourhood cats. Her own cat's nose was pressed to the window, its hind quarters keenly aquiver.

Just before dawn, from the midst of another bad dream, Mel woke to a loud hum, a sharp, electronic ping, the clack of stilettos, the slap of unlaced trainers and snorts of drunken laughter. She grumped through to the kitchen where Bonnie and Joe, the friend who didn't seem to have a home to go to, were piling a dinner plate with slabs of cheese on toast.

How many times have I asked you not to use the microwave at this time of night?

Sorry, the friend mouthed, hamming contrition.

It's not night, Bonnie sniggered. It's already morning!

Yeah. And I have to get up for work in a couple of hours.

Sorry, Joe mouthed again, as the pair staggered out of the kitchen, leaving crumbs, smears of butter and strings of melted cheese on the counter.

Joe was a cheerful, polite lad and it was some comfort that, given Bonnie's age, looks and the outfits she favoured, somebody was there to watch her back when she was out on the town. But in the house, his presence was like one of those invisible electric fences set up between mother and daughter. Mel knew that if she ventured too close, she would be repulsed, painfully.

The next day the chick was still on the grass, looking none the worse for spending the night al fresco. It was making a racket. As its insistent squeals soared to the pitch of a dentist's drill, a sleek adult gull swung out over the rooftops of the tenements, dipped through the pearly dawn, hung, wings beating, above its overgrown darling, and began to deposit squirming morsels into the gaping gullet. It was an awkward exchange, all thrusts and gulps, jabs and grabs but there was no doubt that the gull was doing her maternal duty.

Ears pricked, tail stiff and bushy as a bottle brush, the cat once more whined to be let out.

No. You're staying here. With me.

While Scott was away, Mel had done a lot of talking to the cat but why not? The cat didn't mind, even if he was visibly sulking about not being let out, pawing the floor, raking his claws across the lino and emitting a low, threatening growl. The cat would get over it. His memory was short and he didn't hold grudges, whereas Bonnie had built up a whole barricade of grudges, stretching back into early childhood like a hard-

packed wall of sandbags. Why did Mel persist in attempting
to communicate when she had to check herself before she
opened her mouth? Don't mention that, or that, or that; mind
your tone of voice; don't sigh, frown.

If they could have maintained a cordial silence, skirted
each other's lives like strangers in a boarding house, nodding
as they passed each other in the hall, keeping themselves to
themselves, clearing up behind them as they went, this *phase*,
as Scott insisted was all it was, might pass and mother and
daughter would emerge unscathed. But was it a phase and how
long would it, could it last?

Of course a seventeen-year-old wanted to be off living her
own life. Mel and Scott had no desire to hold Bonnie back.
They were doing everything they could to help her leave home
in the hope that, by helping her go, she'd return in her own
good time, of her own volition, as a sorted, adult version of
the sweet, self-contained child she'd once been. Bonnie had
signed up for some voluntary work on the other side of the
world. Mel and Scott were happy to help out though overseas
volunteering certainly didn't come cheap. But since they'd paid
her plane fare they'd heard no more about her plans. Couldn't
she at least have let them know her departure date, what
progress she was making with inoculations, visas? Shouldn't
she be cutting back on partying all night and sleeping all day;
shouldn't she be sorting out what she needed to do, to take?
Was she having second thoughts; would she change her mind
at the last minute and kiss goodbye to the one opportunity
on her horizon? Her parents, it seemed, would be the last to
know.

At work, Mel spent her day attempting to advise young
people about their plans for the future; young people who
were more than willing to discuss their hopes and dreams.

Not to mention their problems. One lass, a little pixie-faced blonde whose round blue eyes repeatedly pooled with tears, spent two hours chronicling her parents' messy divorce, her involvement with an older man, her struggle to focus on her studies. Mel had listened, offered tea, sympathy and tissues. She'd been patient, supportive and kind but why was it that she knew so much about her students and so little about her own daughter?

She could hear the blaring TV from the street. Bonnie and Joe, still in fluffy pyjamas, were nestled on the sofa.

Hi, said Mel. Hungry?

I'll get food if I want it, said Bonnie.

Hi! said Joe, extra nicely.

Sometimes Mel appreciated Joe's exaggerated sympathy; sometimes, like today, it felt like mockery.

If I'm going to be cooking, I may as well make food for you –

I said I'd get food if I want it, said Bonnie.

One of my students has been near where you're going. She was saying –

Tell me later. I'm watching TV.

You're always watching TV. There's more to life than *Friends*.

It's not *Friends*. You just want to find something to complain about.

I just wanted to tell you –

I don't want to hear what your student said.

Fine, said Mel. Fine. Could you turn the volume down? It will disturb the neighbours.

The neighbours make plenty of noise. You just want to find something to complain about.

Just turn it down, will you? Now.

Mel slammed the door on the screaming sitcom and marched off to the kitchen. This wasn't how she'd meant things to go. On the walk home from work she'd told herself over and over and almost certainly out loud, to stay calm, composed; to avoid any confrontation. She'd failed. Again.

The chick was sunning itself on a brick, its fluffy body puffing over the edges, a look of satisfaction on its well-fed face. As it was a fine evening and conversation with her daughter was now out of the question, Mel thought she'd make a start on weeding the border. She had only taken a couple of steps onto the grass when the twin alarms wailed overhead, the parent gulls swung out over the rooftops and plunged, criss-crossing inches from her face in a blur of beating wings. Bloody birds. Did they ever go off duty?

After a week of the chick commandeering the green, starring the grass with sloppy constellations of shit, of its ever-vigilant parents on double offensive and no improvement whatsoever on her own domestic front, Mel phoned Environmental Health, who said it wasn't their responsibility to remove a chick from the drying green. Under certain circumstances it might be their job to remove a nest, for instance in the early stages of nest building, or if, say, it was blocking a gutter or drainpipe. But as the chick was on the ground, it was – Ha ha! – out of their hands.

She phoned the RSPB, who said their remit was the welfare of gulls in the wild but she might try phoning the RSPCA. The RSPCA said that if the gull was injured, they could arrange for somebody to fetch it and nurse it back to health but otherwise, it wasn't their responsibility. And gull chicks wandering about the place, building up their strength to fly was a normal seasonal occurrence and happening all over the country.

While the feathery-voiced woman elaborated on the developmental process of gulls, Bonnie appeared in the kitchen, scowling, arms folded. Dressed now, and heavily made up. Tarty. No two ways about it.

I need to use the phone, she said.

Just a minute.

Mel couldn't quite believe what she'd been told about the family life of gulls. All those chicks tipped out of rooftop or clifftop nests! One minute they'd be sitting snug in warm abodes made of twigs or moss or plastic – the RSPCA woman hadn't specified what gulls used for nest building – the next, plummet and thud. And what about impediments on the way down; sharp rocks, spiked railings, broken glass? Until then, Mel had imagined that birds knew instinctively what to do when the time came: perch on a branch, take off, flap madly and – hey presto – find their wings and soar.

You're doing this on purpose, said Bonnie.

You'll have to wait. I'm speaking to somebody.

I need the phone now!

Tipping a chick out of the family nest was nature's way of saying it was time to move on but what if the chick wasn't ready to leave? How did the parent birds know when the right time had come?

At that moment Mel didn't want an explanation; she wanted a problem solved.

The parents were the issue, Mel explained, their tactics of intimidation. But the RSPCA woman didn't have any suggestions about how to tackle overly protective parents. She did say that food should not be left out and that it could be several weeks before the chick worked out what to do with its wings.

I need to use the phone! Bonnie snarled. You've been talking for ages!

Do you have to be so rude?

Do you have to be so annoying?

Here, said Mel. Couldn't you have used your mobile?

I don't have any credit! Her daughter snatched the phone and clattered off to the front of the house.

Just remember who pays the bills, Mel said to the empty kitchen.

As a change from talking to the cat, Mel passed on her findings about gulls to the neighbours, who, now that the sun was shining and the grass was cut, had begun to spend more time on the back green. A retired man, plump and fluffy as the chick, who made it his business to dead head roses and assist the Virginia creeper to extend over the fence, admitted to feeding the chick. He'd used his golf umbrella as protection but the parent gulls had torn holes in it; he was happy enough to give up feeding the chick. A single woman, whose downturned mouth betrayed her disappointment with life, made the point that bread attracts rats and foxes and God knows there were enough of them as it was. The bug-eyed parents of a baby girl bemoaned not being able to hang out their washing. A mother of twin boys complained that the lads hadn't been able to play out of doors and were driving her up the wall. A childless couple, who were in the process of trying to sell their flat, commented on the deplorable state of the border though Mel had never seen either of them pull a single weed.

Mel envied the retired man. His children were married; settled, as he put it. As he often put it. She envied the baby's parents their newborn, their newfound, sleep-deprived joy; she envied the twins' mother for knowing where her offspring slept at night; she envied the childless couple their devotion

to foreign holidays; she envied the single woman for having
nothing more to worry about than rats and foxes.

Suggestions were offered as to how to get rid of the chick.

Chase it, scare it away.

Wring its neck.

Now, now. This is a chick we're talking about.

And there are parents present.

Chuck it over the hedge onto next door's green.

Now you're talking.

On either side, the common plots had long ago reverted
to wilderness; nobody ever attempted to hang out washing,
read, sunbathe, garden, play, light barbecues. The mention
of barbecues sparked an irritable flare of comments on the
ruinous effect of sizzling sausages on clean laundry.

The consensus was to relocate the chick but, as the retired
man pointed out, the removal operation would require at least
two people: one to nudge the chick onto a spade and lob it
over the high hedge, another to fend off its avenging parents.
There was the safety aspect to consider. Not to mention the
prospect of making complete fools of themselves. As was often
the case when it came to communal responsibilities, the parley
wound up on a positive note but nothing was done.

Later that evening, Bonnie and Joe went out again, this
time quickly and quietly, offering no information about where
they were going or when they might return. Before going to
bed, Mel checked her email. Another message from Scott told
at some length of another bicycle ride along a riverside path,
followed by details of yet another meal. Did he really think she
gave a damn what he ate? Since he'd been away she had barely
cooked. As Bonnie refused to eat anything she prepared, it
was hardly worth making more than a sandwich for herself.

Scott wanted to know whether things had improved at

home. As they hadn't, she postponed replying, removed
the most dangerous debris from Bonnie's room, once again
switched off the electrical appliances and went to bed. The
chick had stationed itself directly beneath the bedroom
window. It was squealing querulously. Had its parents
forgotten to feed it or abandoned their vigilance? The cat
padded heavily across Mel's bed.

When she checked Bonnie's room the next morning, the
bed was empty. No message on the phone. Mobile number
unobtainable. No clue as to where she might be. Should she
try calling some of the numbers of Bonnie's friends, numbers
she'd gathered surreptitiously, in case of emergencies? Was
she over-reacting? Her daughter was legally an adult. Just. It
was time she learned to step back, wasn't it?

She sent off a long, tense email to Scott, knowing he
couldn't do anything to help but needing to tell somebody,
somewhere. He'd be sympathetic, she could count on that
but sympathy wouldn't solve anything. And sympathy for what
– being useless, redundant? It wasn't as if, like the gull chick's
parents, she'd had to fend off predators. She'd been replaced
in that role.

Scott emailed back instantly, expressing concern and
volunteering to contact Bonnie, give her a talking to, set things
straight about what she should appreciate, be grateful for, not
take for granted. No, Mel replied, he should do no such thing.
Had he forgotten that any kind of reprimand would only make
things worse?

That morning she worked at home, in case Bonnie showed
up. Wasn't it today that she had to go for her inoculations?
She'd already missed an appointment at the clinic and one
at the consulate, related to her visa. At least if Mel was at
home and somebody needed to get in touch, if something

had happened, she'd be there. For all the good she could do, though, she might as well be on the other side of the world.

The chick was padding about on the grass, giving a little hop and awkwardly, one at a time, unfurling its wings.

That's it! she called out. Keep going. Try again. Flap them. Flap, Flap! That's what wings are for! She was shouting, through a closed window, at a bird. But there was nobody to hear or look askance.

Unfortunately, it didn't turn out to be a Eureka moment. The chick gave its wings a brief airing, a half-hearted flap then folded them away. The mother gull dropped by to shove more sustenance into its big baby.

Bonnie dropped by later in the day. She was grey-faced, lank-haired, tight-lipped. Mel tried to explain how she'd been worried, how all she needed was a text, a message on the answering machine, a note, something to indicate that she was still alive. Bonnie mumbled something which might have been Sorry, or Sod off. She took a shower, changed clothes, made herself a sandwich which, for once, she ate in the kitchen. The silence between them, it seemed to Mel, was more wary than hostile. She was about to risk some small talk about the gull chick and the neighbours when Joe arrived at the door and off, once more, the pair of them went.

Days passed. The chick became a bit less fluffy but no more energetic. For hours it sat plumply on the grass, eyes half-closed, soaking up the sun, digesting its last meal and waiting for the next, its curved beak giving the impression of a sly smile. Spoiled brat, Mel thought.

Of course the chick did eventually learn to fly. Mel didn't witness its take-off. One day it just wasn't there. She checked all around the border in case it was lurking amongst the tall weeds; there was no sign of it. And there were no more air attacks. The border was a tangle of neglect but here and there shrubs which had withstood the weather were blooming. Mel began to yank up the ground alder and couch grass, to free a lavender bush from its choke collar of weeds. She heard birds overhead, calling softly to each other, as if they were having a genteel, avian conversation about the lovely weather. High above their temporary nursery, the gull family – sleek white parents and a fluffy grey chick drifted on a lazy, contented loop then, gliding on a thermal between the chimney tops, swung out of sight.

L'Air du Temps

Nothing to be done but follow the invisible threads from the revolving door to the counter, where perfume bottles catch the hot store lights and deflect them like swords made of nothing but coloured light.

There's something furtive in your touch; the salesgirl's head swivels to check you out as you pick up a frosted glass heart with green glass wings and a *Tester* label slapped across the top. The salesgirl, with her flawless makeup, frizz-free hair and crease-free black on black doubts your intentions. Testers are not just for the fun of scooshing free scent on wrist or throat. They are for the serious consideration required prior to purchase, prior to the shelling out of serious money.

You replace the heart-shaped bottle without sampling its contents, pick up others, put them down again. Perfumes for women are contained in sinuous, strokeable receptacles; their names intimate desire, passion. Colognes for men come in

hard-edged, assertive bottles, with straight-shooting names –
Safari, Jazz, Boss. But there's one, an old-fashioned bottle with
an unassuming oval label and a hint of the medicinal, capped
by a tiny gold crown. Its shape does not invite comparison to
any male body part; it suggests nothing but a bottle, with such
a narrow neck that when you unscrew the cap and upend the
bottle, a single, astringent drop dampens your fingertip. Finger
to wrist, nose to wrist. Nose to wrist again and something
almost comes of it, something almost takes shape, the ghost of
a note trembles in the overheated, aromatic air.

But no. Not quite. There's a brief moment when the
swords of light dance and shimmer before they resume their
settled, decorative geometry and it's time to move on, before
the salesgirl with her predatory smile approaches, wanting to
know if you require any assistance.

Historical Dust

On one of those days which never properly get light, just slouch into diluted murk for several hours then slink back into neat gloom, Martine takes an off-peak morning train to the city centre to meet her daughter, Dulcie. It is late November – in retail terms, close to Christmas – and so the dreary outlook doesn't deter the mostly female passengers from gabbing at full tilt about the day's shopping ahead, how many friends and family they have to buy for and how hard it is to find good gifts at good prices.

Martine tends to ignore Christmas shopping until the last minute. Her main reason for the trip is to buy Dulcie – or at least try to buy her – a winter coat. Not before time, if the sorry old thing she shows up in is anything to go by. They have lunch first – well, Martine has lunch and Dulcie has breakfast – in a bustling tapas bar, where the Afro-Cuban beat and the jumping décor, zig-zags of tangerine, gecko green and hot pink, keep the dreichness beyond the door at bay. Dulcie appreciates eating beyond her meagre budget and puts up little resistance to her mother footing the bill.

Workwise, little has changed since they last met up. Martine is still battling against dust, bureaucracy and towering stacks of books, folders and box files. The local history archive she curates is to be relocated, in smaller premises and at a much less user-friendly location. It is not part of Martine's remit to sort and box the thousands of items which comprise the archive, but no-one else is familiar enough with the contents to pack for transportation in a manner which might avoid chaos at the other end. And it's just the way of it that her heavily pregnant assistant can't be called upon to do any lifting or subject her respiratory tract to historical dust. Martine puts up with persistent backache, buys herself a face mask.

Bring on the winter break, she says, as Dulcie tucks into her *huevos rancheros*.

It's okay for you, says Dulcie. I don't get paid holidays.

I know, says Martine. I don't see why everywhere has to close for so long. People need to exercise just as much in winter as the rest of the year.

More, says Dulcie. And they need to earn more too.

Most of Dulcie's income comes from short-term community projects with a focus on health and exercise, which either finish at the year's end or shut down for weeks over the break. It may be well into the new year before she is working again, and who knows how much longer before she'll be paid. Being skint in winter is worse than in summer and there's no denying that her daughter looks peaky. Her complexion is the bluish hue of skimmed milk, hair dull as dead straw. She is living proof of why those who can afford it take themselves off for some winter sun.

They trail round countless clothing stores which cater for
twenty-something women, where seasonal hits blast from
every door. How many more renditions of 'Merry Christmas
Everybody' will they have to endure? Martine riffles through
the rails, fingering fabrics. Though there is no shortage of
flimsy tops and skimpy party dresses, few coats or jackets
have any warmth or substance. Do young people not deserve
to be insulated against the elements? Are they so stoked with
hormones they don't feel the cold?

I think I'm coming down with something, says Dulcie. I so
can't afford to be off sick.

I know, says Martine. Which is why you should wrap up
warmly.

She waits at the entrance to trashed changing rooms,
where disenchanted shop assistants attempt to restore order
to heaps of tried-on-and-rejected garments. Martine maintains
a patient smile and keeps an eye on the clock. Dulcie pops in
and out of cubicles, parades in front of floor-length mirrors,
swithers about buttons and collars and cuffs, colours and
fabrics and cuts, and fails to settle on anything.

Choosing a coat takes time but couldn't she settle on
something that would do for the time being? These days it
isn't as if a coat, a job – or, for that matter, a relationship – is
meant to last. You expect a coat to give at the seams, the
buttonholes to fray. A job has rebranding or redundancy built
in. Martine should know. Early in the new year she has to
reapply for her own job. It has been given a fancy new title,
involves more work and, unsurprisingly, offers less pay. As for
a relationship – hers, it would appear, has exceeded its shelf
life. While she still has a salary and doesn't – yet – have to go
cap in hand to Doug, she would like to buy her daughter a

winter coat.

But perhaps it would be simpler to give Dulcie some cash and let her shop by herself. She is a grown woman, if not an altogether solvent one. But would she choose something sensible and warm? More to the point, would she get around to making any purchase at all, or would she just shunt the money into another channel of pressing financial need?

Bills and rent have to be paid, everyday living costs and unforeseen expenses have to be met – and Dulcie is far from extravagant – but she's crying out for a decent coat, and not just to protect her from the elements. She needs something to wear for the job interviews that have become a dominant feature of her life. It doesn't do to look as if you haven't the wherewithal to brush up for the occasion, even if it's the truth.

By four in the afternoon it is close to freezing point and dark enough to be midnight. Footsore, dispirited by their lack of success, mother and daughter agree to call it a day. They are negotiating a path to the station through the sluggish drift of shoppers when Martine spots a wallet on the wet street. She picks it up; opens it.

Hand it in to one of the shops, says Dulcie. They'll pass it on to the police.

But there's cash, says Martine. Somebody might pocket the cash. This is an expensive time of year. People get into debt.

You don't need to tell *me*.

Are you in debt?

I didn't say that.

But are you? says Martine. Because it's a very bad idea –

I know, Mum.

You hear all these horror stories about debt collectors –

I know! I'm not six!

Martine bites her tongue. A disagreement with Dulcie can

so quickly turn into a full-blown ding-dong. And take long enough to subside.

Do you really think, says Dulcie, that a store manager is going to pocket the cash?

No, no. But you never know with the police.

God, you're such an old hippy.

I am not. And I was never a young hippy either.

I've seen the photos, says Dulcie. You in the kaftan and headband. Dad with the money beads and the Afro. Has he been in touch?

No. It's fine, she says, going through the wallet. Bank cards, bus pass, driving licence, gym card, a student card – that should help – and a membership card for a casino. I'm surprised a student can afford the subscription.

Maybe the student works at the casino, says Dulcie. As a bartender or a croupier. Croupiers get a good hourly rate. They train you up. I might check it out.

Dulcie is always on the lookout for work. Any kind of work.

Don't you have to be a whizz with numbers? And wouldn't it be a very late finish? Think of the cost of taxis home –

Mum!

Yes, you know. Well, the wallet belongs to a guy called Wei-Wei Fang. I should be able to trace him through his student number.

Why are you doing this?

Because a young person, a student, has lost money.

Would you be so keen to track him down, says Dulcie, if you found cards for massage parlours or fetish clubs?

There's nothing like that. And if you lost your wallet, wouldn't you want it back?

Of course I would! It's still weird, you going through a

stranger's stuff.

They continue on their way. It is too cold to stand on the street and bicker. Besides, if Martine doesn't get a move on, she'll have to pay double for a peak-time ticket.

Shortly after Doug walked out, supposedly to *think about things* but in fact to fuck a younger woman who owned a flat in the West End and took home twice his salary, Martine attended a workshop for employees across the region. It was billed as 'an opportunity to increase motivation and boost morale'. For her, a dust-free afternoon and a break from soul-searching were incentive enough.

After putting the attendees in pairs, the workshop leader, a florid, besuited young man, asked them to exchange wallets. As an ice-breaker, they were to compose a thumbnail sketch, based on the contents of their partner's wallet, then share it with the group.

Do we have to? said Martine.

No party poopers allowed! But I can't help wondering, the florid young man added slyly, what this lovely lady might have to hide?

If Martine had something to hide, she would do her damnedest to prevent him finding out what that might be, but she went along with the task. She didn't want to attract further attention. Besides, her wallet contained no awkward surprises: no cards for dodgy clubs, indeed, no cards for any clubs at all. Her plastic was all run-of-the-mill and there were no compromising photos: only a baby pic of Dulcie, when she was gummy and bald, and a faded, creased headshot of Doug, when he did have a sort of Afro.

My ex, she said, when Hayley, whose nubuck wallet contained a glittering sheaf of cards for bijou boutiques, arched a perfectly sculpted eyebrow but was too well-bred to pass comment.

When it came to sharing time, the thumbnails offered few revelations. There was tittering speculation as to the services a 'fairy godmother' might provide and a respectful hush at a contact card for a cancer nurse, but that was about it. The real reason for the session, as attendees discovered during the final presentation of the day, was to prepare the workforce for 'significant restructuring'. Everybody knew what that meant.

On the station concourse, Martine presses some cash into Dulcie's hand and urges her to get a coat, no matter how many unpaid bills she has.

I might wait until after Christmas, says Dulcie. When the sales are on.

That's weeks away. You need a coat *now*.

You'll miss your train if you don't get going.

They hug, briefly. Martine pushes through the turnstile then hurries down the platform, wondering why on earth she is in such a rush to get home.

The next morning, she phones the university where Wei-Wei Fang is matriculated and outlines her reason for calling.

I believe *Fang Wei-Wei* is how we should refer to this person, says the breathy female administrator before enunciating pleasantly but firmly that the university cannot give out any contact details. If Martine might supply her own details, the university would pass them on and the student could contact *her,* if he so wishes. *If he so wishes*? Why would anybody *not* wish to get their property back?

As it is close to the break, the administrator adds, some students may have already vacated their term-time residence.

Would it not be better, then, if you were to give me Mr Wei Wei's details so I can contact him directly? says Martine, despite knowing full well that when it comes to protocol, there is no arguing with any administrator worth her salt.

Snow has fallen overnight and transformed the neighbourhood into a winter wonderland but the furred, glittering gates and railings do little to lighten Martine's spirits. It is Saturday morning. All Doug's remaining clothes are piled on her bed, formerly *their* bed. She intends to sort them into what is good enough for the charity shop and what should go straight to recycling. She keeps thinking and sometimes – *often* – hoping that Doug has left behind so many bits and pieces because he fully intends to come back, that it's just a matter of time before he comes to his senses, realises he misses her unbearably, not to mention the life they've built together, and returns, tail between his legs, vowing to make up for his desertion, heal the heartbreak he's caused, and so on and so forth, running the gamut of reconciliation scenarios.

And yes, she gets a bit weepy at the sight of his abandoned clothes, even though all that's left is the old, worn, and intrinsically crappy: he's already made off with the good stuff. It occurs to her that if Doug were dead, she'd have to deal with all his stuff. Or would she? Perhaps this would now fall to the new girlfriend. Perhaps the new girlfriend would have to decide about Doug's every last sock. Under these circumstances – either making such decisions or being passed over for the task – weeping would be a perfectly acceptable response. But weeping over the unwanted jeans and jerseys, t-shirts and underpants of a husband who, cliché of clichés, has dumped you for a younger model, is pitiful.

When the phone rings she jumps, as if caught out by guilty imaginings. The line is bad. A voice is saying her name but it's hard to make out much more. Assuming it is somebody selling double glazing or claiming she's won a lottery in some far-flung country, she is on the point of hanging up when, some familiar syllables emerge from the crackle. Fang Wei-Wei?

Yah, yah. Fang Wei-Wei.

Oh, she says. Hello!

The reception is poor and Fang Wei-Wei fires out his words but she catches that he is an international student, far from home, and she would be saving him a *very big deal of trouble if he could collect his wallet.* Today.

Okay, she says, thinking about her plans for the day and realising she has none. What time were you thinking about?

Now. I am here already. At your door.

Oh! Just a minute, then.

She runs a brush through her hair, checks her face in the mirror. At least she doesn't look too pig-eyed and ravaged from weeping.

Fang is lean and muscular, which suggests that he makes the most of his gym membership. He has a broad, open face and the flush on his cheeks is overlaid by a sheen of sweat.

Ten thousand thank yous, he says.

He pumps her hand energetically, then shivers. He wears only jogging pants and a sweatshirt. She invites him in. It is far too cold to leave anyone standing on the doorstep. Especially somebody not wearing a coat. He knocks the snow off his trainers and makes fastidious use of the doormat. In the kitchen she offers tea and coffee. He refuses both.

It's all there, she says, handing over his wallet.

He flips through the cards, nods, pulls out the cash. Thirty quid. She checked. A ten and a twenty.

Take it, he says. As a reward.

No, no. Not at all.

Take it!

In between going back and forth – Fang insisting she take the cash, Martine continuing to refuse it – she learns that he is from Nanjing, and studying chemical engineering. He can't afford to go home over the winter break and is homesick for food, heat and family. She doesn't ask about the casino.

I go now, he says.

Once again he proffers the cash. Once again, she refuses it. Just a minute, she says.

In the bedroom she scoops up an old, fleece-lined parka of Doug's and returns to the kitchen. She holds out the parka.

Take this, she says. To keep out the cold. It was my husband's. He's ... gone.

A frown puckers Fang's broad, smooth brow.

Dead?

No, not dead, she says, resisting the melodrama of adding: but dead to me.

He doesn't need it any longer. You'll be doing me a favour if you take it. Please.

No, says Fang. Thank you, no. I must go now.

Deftly returning the cash to his wallet, he makes for the door.

A thousand thank yous, he says. He raises a hand, crunches down the snowy path.

A few days later, a small packet drops through Martine's letterbox. It contains a pair of stuffed, cotton fish. Martine has seen similar items in the windows of Chinese restaurants. There is also a Christmas card, her first of the year. A grinning Santa hefts a sack of presents. Inside the card, in a cramped hand, the words: *Goodluck Fish from Fang.*

She hangs the fish near the living-room window on their tasselled, red silk rope. Heads up, mouths open, fat bellies bumping together. She thinks they might be carp. She knows that in Poland and Slovakia, carp is the mainstay of Christmas dinner but these are from Fang Wei-Wei, who is from Nanjing, and probably mean something quite different from a seasonal meal in Łódź or Bratislava.

The cold weather continues. Snowmen, with carrot noses and beer-bottle eyes, begin to appear in the park at the end of the street. Martine hasn't heard from Doug but has disposed of all his remaining clothes and belongings. It had felt good to be decisive. For a while. Relocating the archive has been beset by obstacles and delays, and her backache persists, as does the stubborn, historical dust.

Dulcie's projects have wound up for the year and nobody is hiring over the festive season, not even for minimum-wage Santa's elves. Dulcie still hasn't got around to buying a coat. The days are shorter than ever but now and again the winter sun bares its pale, insipid face. When a draught skitters through the loose window-frames, Fang's goodluck fish twirl, their sequinned eyes glint. Martine hopes she has hung them in an auspicious position.

Not by Blood Alone

First thing he does is ask for a table, then sits me at it.

Fold your arms, he says. Look into the distance.

Distance? say I. Ain't no distance I can see.

Manner of speaking, says he, leaning in, adjusting my bonnet – fresh-laundered for the occasion – setting a string of rosary beads within my reach, artful-casual. His breath reeks of jugged hare.

A stocky cove he is, plump-cheeked, tricked out in britches and Montero cap, as if he's on a hunting trip and I'm his quarry – which, in effect, I am. He fiddles with his easel and sundry other appurtenances, squints at the window, adjusts his position, and again, to get the best of the light. It's bright out, but no hint of heat accompanies the March sun.

Will people sneer at me for dabbing on a touch of rouge to improve upon my prison pallor? Let them. They sneer already. And all, after all, is vanity.

Turn your head to the side, says he. Fix your gaze on some particular detail.

I see no detail, sir, say I, and stare into the cell's deep gloom.

I can tell he thinks I did for them, throttled the two beldams and slit the young char's throat, to stop them blabbing. I can tell by how he drags the chalk against the page he thinks I'm vile, and will depict me, awaiting the noose, as a brazen hellcat. But if I be innocent, as I have insisted, repeatedly, I am, of what should I repent?

Despite the dire abasement it entailed, I told the court the blood found on my shift was from my monthly flow. I told the court that blood let by slitting another woman's throat could not have found its way onto my undergarments without it also marking my sleeves. I told it all to the court and I ain't for telling it again. To the learned gentlemen of the law, blood was blood, and proof of guilt.

I would that I might take the evidence to my grave but am more like to end up on the slab. Perhaps, thereafter, as bones in an anatomy room. Mr H. will sell his prints of me for sixpence apiece and, forthwith, sketch the mob that comes to watch me hang. All told, from my demise, he'll make a pretty penny.

What This Place Needs

Brenda has lost her luggage. No, the airline she flew with has lost it and she is out of sorts. She is on the U-Bahn on the way into the city centre of Nuremberg with no clothes other than what she has on. Not even, for a four-day stint, a spare pair of big black emergency knickers in her hand luggage. A careless oversight. No makeup or toiletries either, other than a 100 ml. squirt of toothpaste. In the compartment, two sleepy children nuzzle against their silent mother, two African men in identical jerseys nod in time to music on their iPods, and a woman, large like herself, is knitting something dainty and fiddly. There's a smell of pickle and the burnt rubber stink of brake linings.

In the morning she will have to shop, return to her hotel, change into a new, untested outfit, go on the tour then give her presentation. Brenda hates shopping in foreign cities. She hates shopping in a hurry. It's never easy to find clothes

which fit, never mind flatter. Though all she really needs for
her presentation is on her laptop, on her memory stick or in
her head, she is a firm believer that a good delivery requires a
good outfit.

The clothes she has been wearing for the last twelve
hours – loose black trousers and long, concealing top are
crumpled, floppy, give off whiffs of airline food and sweat. She
has no deodorant or cologne – it was that or the toothpaste
– never mind a powder compact to blot her shiny nose. The
credit note from the airline will just about cover one outfit
and personal requisites for the next twenty-four hours. If,
after that, her suitcase is still missing, she will receive full
compensation for the value of her luggage. But why would she
want to buy a whole new travel wardrobe when it has taken
years to put together a colour-coordinated set of long loose
tops and trousers in black, aubergine and chocolate? There
is still a slim chance that her suitcase will be delivered to her
hotel later tonight or even first thing tomorrow morning and
that all will then be well.

Stepping off the escalator from the U-Bahn, Brenda's first
sight of the city is a cobbled square, dominated by a mediaeval
kirche and *turm*. The place is all but deserted. A young woman
with long flaxen plaits and a dirndl skirt pushes a bicycle past
the *kirche*: on the handlebars is a wicker basket festooned with
silk flowers and plastic greenery. Quaint, in a kitschy way. A
thin man with twisted feet hirples across the empty expanse of
cobbles. Not so quaint. The striped Punch and Judy awnings of
the bratwurst stalls are buttoned down for the night.

The sky is a deepening velvety blue. A sliver of moon
hangs behind the tip of the *kirche* steeple. The moon appears
to quiver, like a shiny weighing pan settling into equilibrium.
It is so quiet, she can hear herself breathe; her lungs sound

like creaky bellows. Without her suitcase, she feels unusually light; she imagines rising from the cobbles and floating around the church spire in the manner of a Zeppelin. But Zeppelins are too early. By the time Hitler had begun to stage his mass rallies, Zeppelins had had their day. And when the time came, the city was bombed by Spitfires.

Her grandfather, a wartime pilot, told her this, with a touch of pride, when she mentioned that Nuremberg was her next destination. He fetched the photo from the mantelpiece in the care home. The mantelpiece was purely decorative. No open fires were allowed in the home; they offered too much potential danger to the residents, the staff and to the fabric of the building. He waved the faded photo in front of her, the same photo he showed her every time she visited; a portrait of himself in goggles and flying jacket, young and brave and handsome.

Ninety per cent of Nuremberg was destroyed! he whispered loudly in her ear, as though it were a state secret. Ninety per cent! Then with a tight, anxious grin, took himself, humming, to the window and stared up at the sky. Cirrus, he said. Still snow in the air. Mind and wrap up.

She crosses the square, walks down a street dotted with barely lit *love bars* and lap dancing joints, turns and finds herself in a narrow, deserted alley. On one side is the high dark perimeter wall, on the other a strip of pink-lit plate-glass windows. When visitors see the phrase, 'in the heart of the old town', as she will point out during her presentation, they don't usually equate the atmospheric connotations of the phrase with the red-light district. To properly direct footfall, as she finds herself saying repeatedly, visitors need more accurate information.

Brenda is considered to be a leading advisor on how
to rebrand places with a chequered history. She has met
numerous dignitaries world-wide; she has witnessed countless
renderings of indigenous music, dance and cultural ceremonies;
she has chewed and even recklessly swallowed every kind
of national delicacy, from the weird to the disgusting to the
potentially deadly. She finds it difficult not to preface her cache
of traveller's tales with: When I was in Caracas, Beirut, Kabul
...

It's by no means the first time she has turned a corner in
an unfamiliar city and found herself confronted by an array
of hookers displaying their wares but bang up against the city
wall, in buildings which must once have been stables, where
horses nodded long velvety heads, snuffled into straw and
waited to be put to work, is an unusual location.

Once she's out of the district, she continues through
empty streets until she reaches a little old square near the
river: on one corner stands a traditional toyshop – and toys,
she remembers, are something else for which Nuremberg is
famous. The window is crammed with puppets and character
dolls: Pinocchio, Hansel and Gretel, Rapunzel, Little Red Cap,
who is accompanied by a fun fur wolf. Does the wolf open up?
Does it have a zip on its underbelly from which the gobbled-up
grandmother can be extracted in the manner of a Caesarian
birth? Brenda has never liked fairy tales: too much violence,
too much weirdness.

She crosses the river by a narrow bridge. A lopsided
gingerbread cottage clings to the far end. Above it, a sign
in gothic lettering reads: *The Hangman's Museum: See how
the hangman really lived! Five Euro.* Along the riverbank other
quaint, ancient buildings sag against each other, as if for
support. Sweet-voiced birds are flying home to roost. A

willow dips its branches in the water. She might have stepped back several centuries, to a time long before the history that put the place on the map. But if ninety per cent of the city was destroyed, how much of this olde-worlde Nuremberg is genuine?

Her hotel, when she finds it at the end of a rather drab street, is clean, functional and bland: straight lines, subdued colours, subdued muzak, silk flowers in tall dry vases. The stalks stand amid glass beads, intended to give the illusion of water. Her travel allowance would have covered somewhere more upmarket but Brenda makes a point of booking bargain or mid-price rooms; you need to stay in touch with the bread and butter of the industry. That's one reason. Another is that if you keep your expenses down, you're more likely to be asked back.

The room itself is adequate but by no means luxurious. No bathrobes are provided and the towels are far from ample. Under other circumstances the lack of bathrobe or the size of towels wouldn't have mattered but she is disconcerted to realise that even if she had time to have the clothes she is wearing laundered – which she doesn't – all she could have done, had the fire alarm gone off, was wrap herself in a sheet.

She orders a sandwich from room service, munches as she skims through her presentation notes, then, to attune her ear to the language, switches on the TV. Nobody expects her to say more than a few words in German – English is, after all, the *lingua franca* of tourism – but it never does any harm to make an effort. The programmes are mostly intense talk shows, banal game shows, grim, grainy monochrome footage on the history channels, and soft porn.

She's annoyed at herself for staying in her room like some timid tourist, lacking enough sense of adventure to broach the

threshold of a local hostelry, one of those places with long
trestle tables and blazing hearths where she could order up a
plate of smoky sausages and *kartoffelsalat,* knock back a stein of
beer and sink into noisy joviality. She could call Nora, suggest a
nightcap but hates to appear needy.

Brenda knows a great many people in the industry and
meets new people all the time but work trips tend to be short
and swift, over and done with before anything much has a
chance to develop. You have to act on first impressions, steel
yourself to make your way into, through and, if need be, out
the side door of function rooms filled with strangers. You
have to form instant alliances, to waste no time in finding a
temporary soul-mate, or at least somebody you can bear to
spend an evening with. You have to be able to handle farewells
with dignity, or wit, or speed.

The winter before last, she first ran into Nora, in Reykjavik.
The two of them spent a glittering snowy evening eating
herring and drinking Brennivín. Nora, wee Nora, with her buzz
cut and geeky specs, her tweedy sack of a skirt and granny
cardigan – brisk, bossy, no-nonsense Nora escorted her back
to her hotel, clamped her in a bony little hug then set off
unsteadily down the snow-packed road to her own hotel.

Tomorrow, Nora will also be delivering a presentation. She
and Brenda work for rival companies. Both are keen to secure
a contract, any contract. Tour companies are going under
faster than you can say exchange rate. Along with your sun,
sea and sex, along with your culture, your traditional, nouveau
and fusion cuisine and however many wonders of the world,
there's quite a bit more to throw into the pot: keeping up with
outbreaks of crime or contagious diseases; fluctuations in the
stock market, natural disasters, political uprisings, any one of
which can flare up and wreak holidaymaker havoc. Can a lass

from Luton who left school at sixteen be expected to have a strategy to deal with situations that entire governments fail to get a handle on?

She and Nora were in Reykjavik when Eyjafjallajökull erupted and a dust cloud covered most of the northern hemisphere. Iceland's banks were on the brink of collapse – or had they already collapsed? Brenda is already fuzzy about the order of events. She tries to keep up with international affairs but there's just too much going on, too many places where newsworthy things are happening. It didn't take long, she does remember, before the frothy, optimistic conference presentations hit a layer of permafrost gloom.

Nora's presentation for Reykjavik was provocatively entitled: *What this Place Doesn't Need*. She suggested that there might be other ways to introduce international, short-stay visitors to the culture than serving up a sheep's head on a plate, or a portion of fermented shark, with its distinctive, punch in the gut aroma. Appreciating such delicacies, Nora pointed out, took years, generations. Extreme food, sky-high prices and then a dust-spewing volcano which succeeded in bringing air transport to a standstill for weeks was not a winning combination. Not much you could do about a volcano but you could rethink your menu. The Icelandic hosts didn't get Nora's jokes. They spikily defended their cuisine and, when the dark, volcanic chocolate cake and coffee were served up, they pointedly ignored her. Nora laughed it off but she'd been glad of Brenda's company that night, glad to have somebody to hit the bars with.

Brenda sleeps well enough. She is disturbed only once by late-night carousers and unsettled by the fragment of dream in which she opened a suitcase to find it full of bloody sealskins.

After filling up on a healthy Nuremberg breakfast buffet – fresh fruit salad, cold cuts and cheese, rustic bread and jewel-coloured jams and honeys – she makes for the main shopping area, a grid of thoroughly swept, pedestrianised streets. Blue sky. Sunshine. The shop windows gleam. A department store advertises *Das Mollig Kollektion*. It even has a window display of *mollig* mannequins, with moulded Marcel waves which set them back half a century. The mannequins are clad in tops and trousers in Easter basket colours: primrose, crocus, duck-egg blue.

Optimistically she takes the sleek, humming elevator to the third floor. She is impressed by the extent of the collection – an entire *mollig* floor! – but there's not a single black garment in sight, nor anything in chocolate or aubergine; every garment yodels *spring*! What do people do if they need something subdued – for a job interview, say, or a funeral? Or because they need to go to court, or to be quizzed about a wayward child by a head teacher or social worker?

Today, *nicht schwarz,* says the *mollig* assistant. She is wearing the store uniform, a short, tight-fitting aqua dress with yellow polkadots, and a glossy, *mollig* smile. Colour *gut,* she says. Colour beautiful. The assistant pulls out a selection of outfits. Strong solid colours, broad stripes or busy floral prints. How should Brenda choose between them? Would she rather be a tent, a deckchair or an overgrown garden?

Try. *Gut.* Beautiful, says the beaming shop assistant then spins on her neat, aqua heels, leaving Brenda to the hot, bright intimacy of the changing room.

Most of the stuff she tries on is hopeless, though the fabrics are crisp and light and the cut is generous, but there's one outfit she tries on a second time: a grass green trouser suit printed with giant daisies. She can't help smiling at her reflection; she looks vernal, festive, frivolous.

So! says the shop assistant, ringing up the total. The till has a cheery chirp. *Gut!* Beautiful!

After she has also purchased some underwear, a pair of green leather shoes – has she ever before owned green shoes? – a cherry red lipstick and some other essential toiletries, she hurries back to the hotel, oddly excited. She requests her key at reception. The trim young desk girl stops her:

Bitte, Madame. Your baggage has just now arrived!

Oh, she says. Good. But I'm in a hurry. Could you keep my case at reception until this evening?

Ja? says the girl, shaking her head, adjusting her spectacles. If you wish.

Brenda is not in that much of a hurry. She just doesn't want to have to make any further decisions about what to wear, or consider any ironing. While she was out shopping her room has already been cleaned, the bed made up. Two discs of chocolate nestle on the pillows. She pulls off yesterday's clothes and wriggles into the daisy suit. Can she really go through with this new loud look? Will it undermine her professional reputation for evermore? A bird lands on the window ledge and twitters gaily as she slips on her new shoes and slaps on some bold red lipstick.

Though she has done her homework on the not inconsequential history of the city, she likes to spend a few hours walking around a place, getting a feel for the locale, noting down some up-to-the-minute, first-hand details to give her presentation an edge. Today there's no time for that; she'll have to make do with her memory stick and a new, untried and untested outfit.

At the Dokuzentrum terminus, a welcome party awaits, to a man and woman in neutral monochrome suits, ironed

expressions, manicured hair, clutching their iPads and other
state-of-the-art Notebooks. Even Nora looks alarmingly
crease-free and soberly attired, apart from a pair of huge
hooped earrings which resemble snapped handcuffs. As Brenda
steps down onto the immaculate platform, enjoying the
demure sound of the tram door gliding shut behind her, she
senses a communal flicker of – surprise, disapproval?

I am Gisela, says a sleek blonde with Dietrich cheekbones.
So, we are now complete.

As Brenda is a few minutes late, though only a few minutes,
nothing to get worked up about – and Gisela is pointedly
looking at her watch – she doesn't stop to worry too much
about what the welcome party thinks of her outfit. In fact, she
doesn't feel like worrying at all. In her loud garb she might be a
tourist herself, just nipping out of town on the super-efficient
public transport system for a quick, edifying trip, a sobering
fact-finding trip, undoubtedly, but a trip all the same.

Out of the city centre, there's a cool breeze, a sharp, gritty
smell in the air, like steel dust. A bank of dark cloud is rolling
in.

So, says Gisela, before we go into the Docuzentrum, we
will take a tour of the outside.

Obediently the delegates follow her along a gravel path
between straggly bushes.

Bit of a schlep, this venue.

Yeah. And do we really want to see it?

The Rathaus has a lot more going for it as a venue.

Yeah. Haven't they done wonders with the town centre!

A labour of love, these reconstruction jobs. Have you seen
Gdansk? Warsaw?

We will walk about, says Gisela.

They pass a small, dull lake and a ramshackle fairground,

not yet open for business. Without the romance of the night, of blaring music and strings of coloured lights, the painted rides look shabby. Alsatians pad back and forth, jangle their chains. There's a lingering whiff of fried onions and candy floss.

Dig the outfit, says Nora.

Not too frivolous?

Nah, says Nora, putting a flame to her roll-up. Cheery.

As they walk around the rather boring parkway, Brenda catches sight of her green and white legs, the banks of green and white daisies swaying as she follows Gisela's determined lead along the path. Gisela is not walking at a tourist pace. She would not, Brenda thinks, make a good tour guide. A tourist pace is a languid amble, as if there's all the time in the world to go where you're going, or to simply stand and stare. Gisela is goading rather than guiding.

People never take tourists seriously. Not even the people who make their living from tourists. They're always considered to be a bit ridiculous, pathetic, desperate, looking for something beyond themselves which they can absorb, consume, assimilate, something they can sniff or stroke or swallow, and after a bit of somewhere else they can't wait to get back to their own beds, to draw the curtains on life elsewhere and sink into the warm amniotic bath of what they know, and so don't have to think about. As if that's wrong. As if they're all just brainless sponges.

So, says Gisela, now you see where it happened.

As they round a bend in the path they come upon the rally ground, a great man-made maw. None of the delegates is prepared for the scale of the place, its palpable air of dereliction. Unused for seventy years, weeds push through the cracks in the concrete, the brick walls are discoloured, crumbling. In such a vast, barren space, the small cluster of delegates makes no more impression than a few specks of grit, flakes of ash. In this gigantic parade ground, how many thousands, in unison, saluted and screamed *Sieg Heil?*

This is a part of history, says Gisela, we have to live with.

Dark tourism's on the up.

Yeah. Tours to Beirut, Ground Zero, Cambodia's killing fields. Auschwitz is old news.

Gisela flinches briefly at the mention of Auschwitz, then squares her shoulders and smiles broadly.

I am hoping, she says, that today's guest speakers bring some good ideas.

Gisela draws the delegates' attention to Brenda and Nora who are lagging a bit behind the rest of the group. A tall, grey-clad man takes a photo of them on his phone. Others follow suit; snap the odd couple, the weirdos.

Smile, says Brenda.

No way, says Nora. She scowls for the cameras, lights a skinny roll-up and sucks on it aggressively.

So, says Gisela. Now we go inside.

For an hour or more Gisela escorts them through archive footage: swarms of swastikas and jackboots, massed armies and piles of corpses, bombed-out cities and chisel-jawed stormtroopers, *Blitzkrieg* and *Kristallnacht,* a screaming madman whose last planned rally, before invading Poland, was to have been on the theme of peace.

Are we getting lunch before the presentations?

Hope so. Breakfast wasn't much cop.

Mine was okay. Rubbish coffee, though.

Tried the famous *wurst* yet?

No. How about tonight? Sample the beer too.

Goes without saying.

We have much film footage, says Gisela. Many newsreels.

We do not pretend the past did not happen. We teach our schoolchildren about the mistakes of the past. But for the city to survive, we must have something else to offer.

It is with relief that the delegates exit the dark, crowded walls of the Dokuzentrum exhibition hall to gather in the glass-walled concourse where screens and a podium have been set up for the power point presentations. The delegates take their seats. There is no sign of food or refreshments. Brenda is up first.

The crisp cotton of her loud, frivolous outfit rustles as she moves her arms; it's a pleasant, fresh sound, like grasses shifting in the breeze. She has become too used to the dry crackle of static, of stay-pressed synthetics, of dark acquisitive colours which suck light into themselves.

At Gisela's signal, Brenda prepares to approach the podium.

You'd better have some bloody good ideas, says Nora.

Half Here, Half Where

When it happened, it was so unassuming. You were dizzy but in an airy, fit-of-the-vapours sort of way, your field of vision had a light dusting of snowy static but no hissing, then half of you evaporated – poof! And in its place, in half of *your* place, your *space*, was a simulacrum. You had become half girl (half *old girl*), half ghost.

The evanescing was painless. Disconcertingly so. No wrench of severance, no lightning-bolt schism or residual throb of loss. You didn't reach out to your flighty, fugitive side as if you hoped to corral the blown seeds of a dandelion clock or soap bubbles from a wand. Instead, you stood dead still, hoping that stillness might restore you – to wholeness, equilibrium, symmetry?

It was the day before midsummer. You were standing at a tall window in the cheerful living room of your friend's holiday home, gazing at sand yellow, sky blue and white-capped sea

green. The coastline of France – oh, the romance! – was a
faint smudge on the horizon. Around these parts, perhaps
even just along the road, Turner had painted some of his wispy
seascapes with, according to Constable, 'tinted steam'.

Your reflection in the window glass gave the impression
that your right leg (which appeared as your left) was, in its
share of powder-blue trousers, every bit as solid and ordinary
as its neighbour. Ditto your right arm, extending from the
short, loose sleeve of a t-shirt. Your right side might have been
able to fool a casual observer but it didn't fool you: it was as
insubstantial as steam.

Later the same day. No longer a room with a view but a hot,
crowded, A & E waiting room. There are no visible clues as to
your altered state except that when you embark upon another
trip to the loo, you peg and flop like a half-wooden, half-
rag doll. For nearly five hours you wait, sitting, or propping
yourself against a wedge of wall. There are fewer seats than
patients, a logjam of wheelchairs and no clear path to the
medical bays. You try not to dwell on the sorry state of the
NHS. The reason you are here is that your blood pressure, to
quote the triage nurse, is through the roof.

*Head, shoulders, knees and toes. Eyes and ears and mouth and
nose.* In the continuing absence of a doctor you tap repeatedly
at various parts of your body. Your weaker left side remains
pretty much as before. The stronger, abler, go-to right side,
with the larger, veinier and nimbler-fingered hand – you
can't begin to compute all the fine motor skills you need
that hand for – is numb, weightless, absent. It might as well
be a hologram. Any contact you make with it has to be seen
to be believed. If you raise your right foot from the scuffed
linoleum, it continues to drift upwards of its own accord. This

is seductive rather than alarming, but something tells you this
is the wrong response.

Your brain is not relaying the correct messages but you
really don't want to think about what your brain is or is not
doing; it is hard enough getting to grips with your wayward
body. But what should the messages be and *where are they* –
sequestered in a locked ward of the brain, until you locate,
identify or recognise the key? Perhaps the correct messages
are shambling around some cerebral waiting room, whining
for attention, jostling for elbow room, fretting for their names
to be called so they can sprauchle towards a fully functioning
nurse holding a clipboard who will, if all goes to plan, direct
them to a door at the end of a hitherto unseen corridor.

Keeping Up

Cilla is dreaming of a pirate, of the swashbuckling, buccaneer variety – roguishly handsome, with a luxuriant beard and glinting earring but none of the stink and ingrained filth that are part and parcel of the trade. No eyepatch or knotted headscarf either but he is brandishing some kind of bladed weapon, a cutlass, surely – isn't that what old-school pirates ran with? He is a distance away and yet somehow close enough for her to smell pipe tobacco and seadog rum on his breath. She can hear herself murmuring 'sea-green eyes' when Jancis's querulous voice barges into her dream and dispatches the brigand.

Cilla. Cilla! We're anchoring in ten. If you don't get a move on, we'll have to wait for ever!

If they're anchoring in ten, they're already too late. Everyone wants a place on the first batch of tenders and queues for the escalators will already be dozens deep. Cilla rolls over on her bunk and peers through the porthole of their shared cabin. In the distance, squat, blocky buildings line the quay against a backdrop of parched scrub. At least they won't be spending their shore day *there*.

She'd only meant to close her eyes while Jancis wrapped up her morning flirt with the waiters, not to actually nod off. Cilla blames the food. There is always so much on offer, and quality food at that. The kitchens work round the clock to turn out ever-more tempting dishes and the aroma of freshly baked bread infiltrates the ventilation system at all hours. Though Cilla always sticks to a Light Continental, even on a shore day when everyone stocks up on breakfast, the waistband of her favourite holiday trousers is already beginning to pinch. Jancis, damn her, can tuck into a Full English every day without any change to her coat-hanger frame.

After being marshalled by bumptious, semaphoring stewards onto a packed escalator descending to the lower decks, the two tramp the gangway to their allotted tender where, by means of some sly elbowing, they secure a spot from which to view their approach to *The Jewel of the Eastern Mediterranean*. More queuing and more gangways before Cilla and Jancis, lurching after several days at sea, join the hordes pouring through the archways of the Old Port and onto the paved streets of the medieval city.

The journey from the deck of their cruise ship to Dubrovnik – a distance of no more than a few kilometres – has taken the best part of the morning. Preparations for lunch are underway and the city reeks of grilling meat and fish. Their first stop: queuing at the ATM for local currency; their second: queuing at the adequate but overpriced public toilets; their third: securing a bench in the shade so Jancis can apply sunblock.

You could always cover your arms, says Cilla.

I *could*, says Jancis, but I don't want to.

As ever, Cilla has dressed for comfort and concealment. As ever, Jancis has opted for style: a sleeveless white dress with a gold border at the neck and hem, strappy gold sandals and matching toenail polish. Her colour coordination is marred by blazing epaulettes of sunburn, from lounging too long on the lido the previous afternoon, ogling the ship's all-male dance troupe as they leapt and flexed, rehearsing for the final night's extravaganza.

There'd better not be loads of stairs, says Jancis, squinting through a gold-trimmed visor at a slice of ancient wall glimpsed between rooftops.

Jancis finds stairs difficult. If they'd booked a city tour, a workaround for those with mobility issues would have been on offer but Jancis prefers to soldier on, if not stoically, and kid everybody – including herself – that she's still in her prime.

We don't *have* to do it, says Cilla.

What's the point in coming at all if you don't do the main sights? Who goes to Paris and doesn't do the Eiffel Tower?

I've never done the Eiffel Tower.

But that's just you, Cilla, trying to be different. *Cilla went to Paris and didn't do the Eiffel Tower. Cilla went to New York and didn't visit the Statue of Liberty. Cilla went to Agra and didn't see the Taj Mahal –*

I did see the Taj Mahal. I sent you a postcard.

Did you? Nobody bothers with postcards any more. Must have been a while ago.

It was. Cameron and I were on our honeymoon.

Oh, *Cameron*, says Jancis. Ancient history, then.

Not to me it isn't!

Jancis bats her eyes at a bronzed hunk, smoking in the

doorway of a coffee shop and resolutely ignoring her. She has never married and considers Cilla's twenty-five-year marriage and ensuing decade of chaste widowhood a huge yawn. Though Jancis's own life – if her version of events is to be trusted – has been awash with steamy and at times stormy affairs, she shows little sign of abandoning hope that some Prince Charming may still rock up and sail off with her into an incomparable sunset.

The two women have been friends for fifty years. Not always the very best of friends but, despite jags of rage and erosive irritations borne of long familiarity, their lives now peg along on similarly solitary lines and, since Cilla became a widow, they've taken their annual holiday together. They've done self-catering cabins, budget packages, city breaks and bus tours but as this year is something of a watershed, they've splashed out on a cruise. It's a pity, they agree, that their budget hadn't stretched to single cabins.

I so want to do the wall, says Jancis. If only my stupid feet are up to it.

Perhaps we need a Plan B, says Cilla, leafing through her guide book. *The cathedral has paintings by Dalmatian and Italian artists, including one by Raphael.*

If they only mention *one* Raphael, nothing else will be worth bothering with.

The reliquary contains the head and a leg of a thirteenth-century saint.

Who wants to see creepy old body parts?

The maritime museum hosts a fine collection of seahorses.

Fun for five minutes, says Jancis. Which way to the wall?

Cilla indicates the slow procession of crumpled shorts, bulging bum bags and floppy hats – no longer an invading horde but a vast herd of docile cattle, plodding across flagstones buffed to a sheen by centuries of feet and hooves, shod or not. The streets are so congested it's hard to appreciate the mix of Gothic, Baroque and Renaissance architecture for which the city is renowned. In the main square, in front of an ornate town hall, a band of men in white shirts, black trousers and crimson cummerbunds is singing in doleful unison to a loose horseshoe of audience.

Klapa, says Cilla. They sing about tragedies at sea, lost love and such.

Oh, let's not stop for the doom and gloom, says Jancis. They'll be passing round the hat in a minute and I don't have any coins.

As soon as they pass through the ticket booth and begin to climb the first flight of steep, uneven stairs, the heat hits them. Jancis, who insisted on leading the way so she didn't have to play catchup, gasps at every step. Cilla's heart begins to thump assertively. She, too, must pace herself. She presses against the sun-baked stone to let a group of neat, nimble Japanese matrons squeeze past. Jancis, oblivious to the tailback, continues upwards. Perhaps she doesn't hear their gentle twittering. Jancis is quite deaf but refuses to admit it.

When they reach the ramparts, the Japanese group patter past Jancis. Cilla catches her breath, takes in the shimmering expanse of sea. Jancis, groaning, massages her ankles.

Couldn't they have got us here before it was so hot?

What a view! says Cilla.

The colour of the sea's a bit wishy-washy, says Jancis, standing on tiptoe so she can see over the perimeter wall. Reminds me of that mouthwash of yours. By the way, I used some this morning but I don't care for the taste.

Bring your own, then.

Surely, Cilla, you don't begrudge me a capful of

mouthwash?

That's not the point.

The point is that Jancis crams every beauty product imaginable into her toilet bag but forgets some essential item, like soap or toothpaste. Always.

The sky is unbroken blue. It is almost noon and fiercely hot, with only the thinnest slivers of shade. Encrusted with tourists, the diamond-shaped ramparts encompass domes, steeples and pitched roofs; the seaward sections run along the top of sheer cliffs. *The walls were built in the thirteenth century to protect the city from invasion, Cilla reads. In the fifteenth century, numerous towers were built upon them; some are still standing.* There's one! she says, gesturing to where the Japanese women are arranging themselves for group photos, their laughter dipping and darting.

Spare me the history lesson, says Jancis. My God, look at all those stairs!

We don't have to go all the way round.

But if we don't go all the way round, we haven't really *done* it, have we?

Does it matter? says Cilla.

It matters to me, says Jancis.

The taverna where Jancis insists they have lunch – persuaded by the moustachioed hunk touting for trade at the entrance – is heaving, but it does have the advantage of terrace seating beneath a vine-laden trellis.

I never want to see that wall again, says Jancis.

But we did it! says Cilla. And you have to admit the views were sensational.

My feet are killing me.

Shall we treat ourselves to wine?

If you say so, says Jancis, though God knows what the local

stuff is like.

They have Italian wines as well.

No, no, says Jancis. When in Dubrovnik –

When the waiter – yet another Adonis – arrives, Jancis quizzes him about the wine list, only to settle, eventually, on a carafe of house white. Having read that sharing plates are the norm, Cilla enquires about portion size but, despite his eloquence on the wine list, the waiter is vague. Not that it matters. Jancis has set her heart on the local speciality – squid ink risotto – and so Cilla, who's allergic to seafood, has no alternative but to order something else.

This is just another tourist trap, says Jancis. Do you see any locals eating here? It can't possibly be *authentic*.

You chose it.

We were hungry, Cilla. We had to eat *somewhere*. I'd just have liked to eat somewhere *authentic*.

Do you think they'd have such hot waiters in an *authentic place*? Or linen tablecloths, traditional music? *If you want the real deal,* the guide book says, *expect a surly proprietor, Formica tables and blaring MTV.*

You're such a smart-arse, says Jancis. And I bet that guide book is way out of date.

Like us? says Cilla.

Speak for yourself, says Jancis. I keep up, Cilla. I keep up.

The wine arrives promptly, the food tardily. Thirsty from so much walking in the heat, both women drink deep.

I don't know why you have to bang on about portion size, says Jancis. Anyone can see you don't exactly starve yourself.

You eat as much as I do, says Cilla. A lot more, in fact.

Maybe, Jancis preens, but I can get away with it.

Do you have to be such a bitch?

I just tell it like it is, Cilla.

Don't bother. I know how it is.

The wine has gone to their heads. They are talking too loudly. Not that it matters; everybody is jawing away and drowning out the weeping strings. The food eventually arrives and the portions are enormous. Jancis wrinkles her nose at the purplish-brown mound on her plate, samples a forkful suspiciously and, loudly enough for half the terrace to hear, pronounces it revolting. She summons the waiter – there really is no need for the finger-snapping – and tells him to take it away.

You want something else?

No, dear, she says, stroking the waiter's smooth, golden forearm with a mottled claw. My friend doesn't like big portions. We can share her dish – can't we, Cilla?

With a shrug, the waiter departs, skinny hips slaloming between closely packed tables, the rejected plate of squid ink risotto held aloft.

By the time they have polished off Cilla's more-than-ample chicken salad, drained the carafe of wine and paid the bill, the terrace is all but deserted.

We're running a bit late, says Cilla.

Just a quick look?

It'll have to be quick.

Tipsily, they veer off the main drag and plunge into a web of backstreets, only to find that the gift shop shutters are drawn, their doors and grilles bolted. Nobody's around. The only sign of life is a slit-eyed cat, basking on a dusty windowsill.

I thought you said they don't do siesta here, says Jancis.

They don't. Maybe it's some kind of local holiday.

So, we're not going to get any souvenirs? I promised my yoga teacher I'd bring her some lavender oil.

She'll cope, says Cilla, opening up her map. I don't think

we're going the right way. We have to work out where
we are, and which direction we're facing, before we go any
further.

But we can't be late back! says Jancis, a rattle of panic in
her voice. The tenders won't wait. *No exceptions*, they said. *No
exceptions!*

I'm trying, says Cilla, to prevent us being late. We could
have asked a local shopkeeper for directions but, as you can
see, there aren't any shopkeepers to ask.

That's a fat lot of use, then! says Jancis. But I wouldn't trust
a local, to be honest. Remember that bus driver on Crete?

It was Corfu.

Same difference. That bus driver screwed us around on
purpose, says Jancis. Bastard. I bet he bragged about it to his
pals in the Ouzo bars.

I'm sure he had better stories to tell, says Cilla.

At the end of their week in Corfu, which until then had
been remarkably hitch-free, they'd decided to save on the
shuttle and take a municipal bus to the airport. The guide book
had made it seem straightforward enough but despite asking
the driver to tell them when to get off, the bus clattered past
the airport and was several miles down the road before they
realised that they'd overshot their stop. They had no choice
but to lug their suitcases off the bus, drag them across the
road and wait amid maize fields teeming with locusts for a bus
from the opposite direction to return them to the airport. It
was quite a wait. They only just made their flight.

Come on, Cilla. We don't have time to stand here while
you ponder that map.

We don't have time to take a wrong turning.

Oh, for God's sake! I told you we should get somebody to
put Google Maps on our phones.

But we don't know how to use the App, says Cilla. And
you said it was more trouble than it was worth. *You said* you'd
rather rely on common sense –

  I don't remember saying anything of the kind, says Jancis,
but we really must get up to speed on technology if we're to
survive in the modern world. I mean, *you* can't even operate
a self-service checkout, can you, Cilla? *You* need somebody to
help you buy a loaf of bread! You should have asked that boy
of yours to set us up with Google Maps. You're always banging
on about what a whiz he is with techy stuff. What's the point
in having children if they can't help out when you need them
to?

They are standing at a fork in the road. Cilla folds her arms.
Jancis digs her knuckles into bony hips. Their mismatched
shadows – one short and skinny, the other tall and stout – are
cast across the intersection, like a female Laurel and Hardy
squaring up for a scrap.

If we're late, they'll go without us! Jancis bleats. They'll
hand over our passports to the ship's agent and we'll be left
high and dry!

Could be worse, says Cilla, at least we have our credit
cards. But the thought of missing the boat, of having to
negotiate repatriation with Jancis, and she's breaking out in
sweat. Her chest tightens. A glittering confetti invades her field
of vision. Is it the wine? Is she having a panic attack, a stroke?
She takes several slow, deep breaths, blocks out Jancis and
her bleating, and concentrates on a plain dark door until the
confetti begins to evaporate and her pulse rate subsides.

Cilla has never been great at map-reading and the print is
so tiny it's barely legible, even with her new glasses. The sun
bites into the back of her neck as she compares the branching
backstreets with the street plan.

Maybe Jancis is right: if they'd had Google Maps, a mechanical voice would be issuing instructions on which way to turn and how long it would take to reach their destination. Hot, tired, footsore and not a little anxious, they might have found the default voice annoying but they could have relinquished responsibility and tottered on, trustingly, without making decisions or bickering or having to think.

Okay! she says, I've got it. It's this way.

Are you sure? How can you be sure?

If we leg it, we should get there in time. Just.

Can't we just take a taxi?

We're in a pedestrian precinct, Jancis. Do you see any taxis? The whole city centre's a pedestrian precinct.

But I'm so tired! My head hurts. And my feet! Oh, my poor, stupid feet –

Just one push, Jancis, says Cilla. It can't be far.

Cilla hopes that she will never again find herself at this crossroads: its crooked sheaf of street signs, its closed doors and shuttered windows, pitted mediaeval walls and time-smoothed paving stones. She sets off. Every so often she glances over her shoulder to check that Jancis, her friend of fifty years, is keeping up.

Rhoda, Blondie

I hear them before I see them: thudding trainers, whoops and guffaws, tons of swearing. Blondie, with the slight, dark-haired lad she often has in tow, leads the way. Whether he's her sidekick or squeeze is hard to tell. When he stretches a hand towards her shoulder – she's near a head taller – she swats it away like a gnat or a sandfly. Not that you can read anything into the gesture: with this lot it's all swat and slap.

They're not supposed to be touching at *all*. They're breaking the rules, as Rhoda says every time her visits coincide with them rampaging down the lane and playing havoc with the beech hedge bordering my garden. That hedge was lush in the spring but since the lane's become a rat run for the wild bunch it's taken a beating.

Rhoda's itching to give the kids a piece of her mind – about road safety, social distancing and anything else she can think of. A good scare will teach them a lesson, she says. Rhoda's very keen on folk being taught a lesson – and getting what's coming to them. She couldn't care less about my hedge but can't abide having her access blocked when she comes to drop off my groceries, can't abide having to wait for the kids to shift before she can nose her Silk Blue VW Golf up to the gate. I tell her she'd best leave well alone; she'll only get a mouthful of abuse for her trouble. Not that my daughter pays any attention to what I say.

Blondie's long, wheat-yellow hair ripples in the breeze. She's tanned – a natural honey rather than the burnt brick spray bake so many go in for these days. She's leggy, in fringed white cut-offs and a black crop-top. On some, the expanse of skin on display would look tarty but Blondie has the poise to carry it off. She's close to full bloom, and knows it. Knows too that the power this gives her won't last, and has no intention of letting the moment pass her by without turning it to her advantage. Takes after her mother, Jewel, in this respect.

Jewel was one of my students. I don't remember all my students – who does? – but some lodge in the mind and refuse to shift. There was a summer when Jewel lived up to her name and dazzled the lads, in school and out. And then there she was, in her final year of school – pregnant. The father had completed his apprenticeship, was already in work and, as such, considered something of a catch. But soon after the baby was born – I'm talking weeks rather than months – he hopped it down south with her best friend and Jewel began to lose her sparkle. Once in a while she came to class – in my day schools had better child-care than people imagine – but her heart wasn't in it. This isn't always the way of it; some of my best students were schoolgirl mums. Motherhood sparked a determination to rise to its many challenges and make a damn good go of it – and a keen interest in nutrition and healthy living. Jewel took another road. Rhoda's seen her up by the war memorial with the other junkies, pacing and jittering, waiting for the man.

It's hot. Some of the lads have their tops off and even the big lad has swapped tracky bottoms for baggy shorts. Perhaps they'll stop at the boatshore for a dip. As usual there are twice as many boys as girls but it's always Blondie who calls the shots, chooses what to do, where to go and who to harass. They must be first or second year of secondary, if there were any school to go to. Girls that age – around thirteen – are much of a muchness but boys, in every respect, are a mixed bag: some are like bolted leeks; some are broadening out and squaring up to the world; others, despite their foul-mouthed swagger, are still wee boys. And every one of them is self-conscious as hell.

Rhoda detests what she calls my *sweeping generalisations*. Though I taught Home Economics for thirty years she thinks I know nothing about adolescents – or that whatever I *do* know no longer matters. People are more enlightened than in your day, she says, as if *my day* were back in the Dark Ages. I may be getting on, and not as nimble on my pins as I was, but I didn't switch my brain off when the pay cheques stopped.

I pay attention. I know my way around a computer as well as her. I'm perfectly capable of ordering my groceries online but she's adamant I need daily face-to-face interaction if I'm to keep my wits about me. I read, I tell her, and a damn sight more than she does, I might add, though with the library and the charity shops closed I'm getting short on books. But when was Rhoda ever bothered about the likelihood of me going gaga? Last winter, when I was bad with the flu, she came by once in three weeks. Now I can't keep her away.

I'm grateful she does my shopping, even if I have to endure the trials and tribulations of her supermarket experience: how Joe Public wasn't wearing a mask, how Jane Public coughed right in her face, how Jim Public was right up her back with his trolley, blah-de-blah. But what really ticks me off is her editing my shopping list, taking it upon herself to cut back on my supply of red wine, full fat cheese and chocolate. What gives my daughter the right to control my consumption? Unlike some that are at the Chianti, the cheddar and the Cadbury's from breakfast to bedtime, I know my limits. At a time when we're all so short on creature comforts, why deny your old mum a treat or two?

And then there are her substitutions: granary bread, though I've told her the grains get stuck in my teeth, and organic carrots complete with lumps of mud. Can a former Home Ec teacher not be trusted to eat a balanced diet? I make myself proper meals: scrub the tatties, steam the broccoli, grill the fish. None of that freezer-to-microwave nonsense for me, which is more than Rhoda, queen of the Dine-in Special can say. But why pay for mud? And if, after all this, I'm spared, how many extra years will granary bread or dirty carrots give me?

I was never a curtain-twitcher before all this started but what can you do if you're ordered to stay at home? Everybody's at it. Mandy next door's up at her dormer window with the binoculars again, and you can be sure she's not bird-watching. We crossed paths on our walks the other day. Would you believe she was out in her pyjamas? *Leisurewear,* she called it, nailing me with her habitual glare and daring me to disagree. Didn't I know leisurewear was the new normal? She reeled off the names of everybody round our way who'd had a 'house party' – a term which now covers anything from two pals having a quiet cuppa to a full-blown hoolie. If anonymity could be guaranteed – though there's a fat chance of that around here – Mandy would shop every last one of them.

The kids are bunched up at the end of the lane, nudging and shoving, spilling off the pavement and charging towards the shop, oblivious to the fact that they're crossing a road. There may be hardly any traffic but there's still *some*, and drivers still need the same time to brake as they ever did. The doorbell jangles like Mandy's wind chimes in a storm as they clatter into the shop.

The kids do the same circuit every day, often twice or three times though, like everybody else, they're only supposed to leave the house *once a day*: from the lane to the corner shop; corner shop to the old harbour; harbour to the boatshore, which at high tide forms a natural pool; boatshore to the Heritage Gardens of the Big House. The deserted marquee, hired for all those weddings the Big House had to cancel, is one of the few places they can still congregate if it's raining. Stan, the gardener, mutters about the mess of fag ends and cans they leave behind but he's a mild man who cares more about the welfare of his plants than his principles, and will go out of his way to avoid any kind of confrontation. After the Heritage Gardens, they troop through the cul-de-sacs of the new builds and then, if they're still restless, it's back down the lane again. I haven't a clue who's up in the new builds. When Bob was alive, I knew all the neighbours, but those days are long gone.

As for the shop, I used to call in regularly for milk and the papers but for the time being – and who knows how long this might be – Rhoda has banned me from going in. It's far too poky, she says. And too poorly ventilated. True, the windows are never open. I feel bad staying away: the Singhs are decent folk and, from the hours they work, must need any business they can get but perhaps, under the circumstances, Rhoda has a point.

With the kids in the shop, it's quiet again, peaceful. Just the swish of Mandy's pampas grass, the blackies and yellowjackets twittering around the hedge, the hum and crackle of the generator up the back. With so few vehicles on the road the air is sweeter, cleaner. There used to be a steady stream of traffic from dawn till dusk but it's dropped off to no more than a trickle. Several bus routes take in the coast road, and tradesmen choose it over the highway for local destinations, but the buses are on a skeleton service and, as most tradesmen have been furloughed, white vans are few and far between. There's no shortage of cyclists, all the same – more than ever, and runners have also taken to using the road when there's a perfectly good pavement for the purpose. You should hear what Rhoda has to say about runners on the road.

A lot more police about too, or maybe it just seems that way because there's so little else on the roads. Up at the roundabout near the highway, they've started flagging folk down. Yesterday, Rhoda was stopped on her way here. I was given a blow-by-blow account of her experience. No, she didn't have to get out of the car, in fact she was told *not* to get out of the car but to roll down her window instead, and no, the officer asking where she'd come from, where she was going and the purpose of her journey did not stick to proper social distancing. She was going to ask him to step back a pace or two but thought better of it. Didn't want to put his back up. All the same, she said, the police should be setting an example, practising what they preach.

Being stopped by the cops was Rhoda's excuse for being half an hour late. I don't see how the delay could have lost her more than a couple of minutes unless she chose to dally with the officers of the law. For all her carping, Rhoda does like a man in uniform, though she's not had much luck in that department – or, for that matter, with men in general. And the current situation must have knocked any dating opportunities on the head. Not that she ever tells me the first thing about her love life, and I'm certainly not daft enough to ask.

She's late again today, which is nothing new. It's not as if my diary is jam-packed with Zoom meetings as she claims hers is but I do like to know what's happening when. If I'm expecting Rhoda, I just can't settle to anything: no time feels as dead as the time I spend waiting for her to show up. Her phone's off, as per usual. I do wonder how long it might take to get hold of her if I *did* have an emergency.

I don't feel the need for a daily visit. Once or twice a week would be plenty, and spacing out visits might give us more to talk about. Maybe it's Rhoda who needs frequent face-to-face interaction but why make out it's for *my* benefit? Since she's been working from home, she hasn't any office gossip to spread and so, apart from belly-aching about rule-breaking, she's down to opining about soaps and reality TV shows. As our viewing choices hardly ever overlap, this doesn't have much mileage. We've never gone in for the heart-to-heart stuff; why start now? To be fair, I don't expect anybody's conversation has much to recommend it at the moment. Even the radio and TV presenters, whose job it is to *create interest,* are picking over the bones of the same old stories time and again.

I miss driving. After I retired, I used to love pootling around the web of backroads, going whichever way took my fancy: you wouldn't believe the number of backroads there are in these parts, linking blink-and-you'd-miss-them hamlets, their straggles of low cottages with hollyhocks up to the eaves. I'd have the windows open so I could savour all the smells of the countryside: the flowers, crops, animals – even a whiff of fresh manure can have its appeal. I'd pass vast green and gold fields, dense pockets of woodland, grass verges teeming with wild flowers. All so close yet, under my own steam, so inaccessible.

Rhoda has offered to take me on a drive, a *short* drive (despite being against the rules), but I'll only get in a car with my daughter behind the wheel if there's no alternative. It's as if she's locked in battle with all other road users, not to mention the road itself – the junctions, roundabouts and traffic lights, as if everybody and everything were conspiring to prevent her getting where she wants to go in the time she wants to take.

It was touch and go whether I'd walk again so I value the use of my legs. And with the current crisis in care homes, I'm more than happy to be in my own place, but when I think of how many batches of scones and pots of lentil soup I'd see to completion in an average working day, how many worksheets on The Alimentary Canal and Hygiene in the Home I'd mark, my days now seem so slack, empty. Sometimes, if the weather's bad, the sanity walk is done and dusted first thing, and another long day indoors looms, I close my eyes and try to visualise one of those country roads – in sunshine, always in sunshine. I never quite get beyond the here and now: I'm too aware of my old backbone pressing against the slats of a kitchen chair, my slippers sliding around the worn lino.

Still, one good thing to come out of this fine kettle of fish is that I'm out on the coastal path rain, hail or shine and, as somebody else usually has the same idea, there's the prospect of a nod, a smile, a word or two. Who'd have thought that exchanging pleasantries with a stranger or passing acquaintance would become the high point of my day! There are always some who can't or won't meet your eye, who let their gaze slide over the rocks or swing out to sea but most will greet you, however briefly. It's a wonder how much the sound of another's voice can lift the mood.

That's them leaving the shop now. Mr Singh pokes his head out of the door then retreats inside as they hare off towards the old harbour. Blondie and the dark-haired lad scramble onto the breakwater and bound along the wall to the pierhead. The lad sweeps Blondie up and dangles her, kicking and screaming, over the basin then pulls her back to safety amid raucous cheering. The pair spring down onto the quay and they're all off again, belting towards the concrete clubhouse of the Royal British Legion, with its flaking, painted Saltires. Next stop the boatshore?

Rhoda's even later than yesterday. To stop myself clock-watching and getting out of sorts, I pick up my book, a historical adventure about an old soldier being pursued from one end of the country to another by an adversary. I'm about a hundred pages in. It's a good story, well told, but after a bit the heat begins to make the print swim.

I'm jolted awake by shouts, squealing brakes, a blaring horn followed by a deep silence. I get up from my chair, wiggling my toes to get the feeling back, blinking until my vision clears. Unsteady, I go to the window. The physio told me not to move quickly after being stationary; my balance has never been a hundred percent since the stroke. If Mandy has her binoculars trained on my living room, she'll think I've been on the Rioja.

I can tell straight away that it's Rhoda's Golf skewed across the road, back end pointing towards the shop, Rhoda's head slumped on the dashboard, Rhoda's hands – the hands of my

only daughter – gripping the steering wheel. A pace or two
from the front passenger door, Blondie's limp body lies half-on,
half-off the pavement: feet and legs on the pavement, torso,
arms and head on the road. The dark-haired lad, crouched
on the road, is stretching a hand towards Blondie's shoulder,
hoping against hope that she'll swat it away.

Signed Copy, As New

Dear Rosemary,

This not your real name, of course, nor even a pen name
– which, to my knowledge you've never used – but we can
never be too careful, can we? I took the name from a shrub
I remember from your walled garden. Rosemary is hard to
grow so far north yet in that sunny, sheltered spot it thrived.
And then there's the literary allusion: 'rosemary, that's for
remembrance', as poor, distracted Ophelia mused.

It may surprise you that I can still remember your postal
address but Far Point House, Windblown Bay, is nothing if not
memorable. People so rarely write letters these days, never
mind getting down to the business with the envelope and the
stamp, not to mention locating a pillar box into which to pop
the finished article, but, on this occasion, pen and paper fit
the bill. As it happens, I'm using my trusty signing pen, which

must be at least as old as our acquaintance! Few can stomach a lengthy email and I would hate to try your patience. As I recall, you can – or *could* – be rather wanting in the patience department. Besides, I no longer seem to have your email address on my system.

As a somewhat famous writer, you are bound to suffer many more wearisome obligations, commitments and sundry intrusions on your time than I, yet I too have my modest share. How such things conspire to keep us from what we love most – exploring the forking paths of our own fictional gardens. I don't mean to needle you, only to give your memory a gentle jog.

I am writing this in the small hours. I am no longer the night owl of old but a born-again morning person: lover of the slow seep of daybreak and birdsong for breakfast. I turned in around midnight but tossed and turned and rearranged my limbs over and over. I couldn't quite put my finger on the cause of my disquiet but, in the hope that a good read might nudge me into the land of nod, I made a start on your new novel. Alas, it did not engage me as I had hoped it would, and put it aside after the first chapter. Given the rhapsodic reviews it has received, the problem must surely lie with me.

When my baffling indifference abates, I fully expect to appreciate what all the fuss is about. Nevertheless, eight hundred pages is a hefty commitment, particularly when the typeface is so small and cramped. Issuing from such a prestigious publishing house, I was disappointed that the page design wasn't more appealing, though such decisions – frustratingly, wouldn't you agree? – are almost always beyond our control.

Earlier this evening – no, it's *yesterday* evening now – I attended your session. I sat discreetly at the back. The seating was, as ever, rickety and uncomfortable, and a heavy smell of lentil soup hung in the air. You were on in a church hall normally used for parish council meetings and the table tennis club. It is one of the smaller venues – the smallest, in fact, of the hotchpotch of halls and club rooms that, for one week a year, are given over to our book festival. The larger venues are always given to the big hitters: hard- and medium-boiled crime, historical romance, cookbooks flash-fried by celebrity chefs. People here know what they like, and what they don't. Nothing under the banner of *experimental fiction* is likely to cut it with local readers – but hey, you were sold out!

It was a good enough event though it beats me why the over-excitable host, a young man labouring under an all-too-audible head cold, chose to impose garble and feedback on us when there was no need at all for amplification. You were wise to ditch the mics from the get-go. I must say, it took me back to hear your voice again. To my ear, it hasn't changed at all over time. Some do. The voices of smokers drop in pitch, degenerate in clarity and become raw and rasping, as if their vocal cords have been dragged along a dirt road. And you are a smoker. Or were. *A very heavy smoker.*

I too used to be a smoker but a lightweight in comparison to you. I quit a few years back. Doctor's orders. It's hard to tell whether quitting improved the quality of my voice but at least I still *have* one and, mercifully, that grim period is behind me. One possible outcome of the condition or its treatment was that I might lose my voice completely, and permanently, and be reduced to communicating, Dalek-like, by way of an electrolarynx. That, as I'm sure you can imagine, was no small concern: more than ever the voice has become an essential tool of our trade.

When we tapped away on our Olivetti or Smith-Coronas,

accompanied by clacking keys, line-end pings and the oh-so-satisfying clicks and swishes of the carriage return, who knew that every so often we'd have to forsake the fug and clutter of our huts and attics, our boltholes and box rooms, brush up and sally forth to confront that wayward beast – *the reading public*? We must read our work aloud. Worse, we must *talk* about it, and respond to the baggy or convoluted questions beloved of certain festival-goers, questions that require a full disquisition to do them justice. We must cut these behemoths down to size, crunch our judgements into a couple of smart and sparkly sound bites. Off the cuff. Never mind that our habit may be to ruminate on each and every word.

To your credit, you were neither glib nor prolix in the Q&A, and handled the audience deftly, if ducking and diving a bit when the chap in the tartan waistcoat asked whether the sex scene involving a deerhound was based on personal experience, and the wispy woman in chartreuse carped about why you gave so few of your female characters a happy ending.

All the same, I did wonder why you felt the need to describe yourself, and your urge to write, as 'a little bit crazy'. Why perpetuate the shibboleth of the mad artist? Why link the *partly* pleasurable act of creation with the wretchedness of mental illness? The host was only too happy to run with your 'little bit crazy', even citing your 'alternative look' – inappropriately, to my mind – as evidence that you stand apart from the dull and predictable, the stodgy, the sane. And that this, somehow, is the key to your artistry. Between the sniffles, I even caught the word 'genius' in his laundry list of superlatives. But really, how could you abide his bootlicking?

A very heavy smoker. Would you believe I can remember where and when you spoke those very words? We were on the terrace of your lovely house on the island, dragging

enthusiastically on our fags and supping your peaty home
brew. Our tumblers stood on a rustic but beautifully finished
table which your rustic but beautifully finished husband had
fashioned from driftwood. It was one of those mild, still
evenings peculiar to the north, when the air is fragrant and the
light a shimmering caress, when waves lap the shingle, a lone
gull soars and all seems right with the world.

It's twenty years since we last met yet I had no trouble
recognising *you*. I was well-primed, and had the opportunity
to observe you – intently, intently – throughout your
presentation. In the festival bookshop, inching forward in the
modest but decidedly sluggish queue for the signing table,
I experienced a qualm or two. Our looks have changed, of
course. You've gone from bum-skimming, Pre-Raphaelite locks
to a hennaed urchin cut. I've gone the other way. I used to
wear my dark hair cropped but it's been silver and shoulder-
length for more than a decade. A change of hair colour
and style can be an effective disguise: think of all the screen
fugitives who still give pursuers the slip by donning a wig. And
there's no denying that I've put on the beef, which might have
thrown you. But not a glimmer of recognition, when close
observation is a writer's bread and butter?

When you were last in town, you came over for lunch. You
were checking out care homes at the behest of an elderly aunt.
As you didn't know the area, a fellow writer, Donny Burke –
nice guy, nasty books – had put us in touch. I heard he gave
up writing and went into mediation, believing it to be a better
outlet for his observational skills. Your aunt was dismayed
by the going rate at our local care homes and decided not to
relocate after all, so there was no reason, until now, for you to
return.

I stood at the signing table. I told you my name which, like yours, is also my writing name. Nothing. I mentioned your visit. How my crabbed old cat took a shine to you, purred on your lap and proffered its pale throat for tickling. I believe it even licked your wrist with its scratchy tongue. Again, nothing. You wore a purple sack dress. Twenty years on, I can remember your clothes! It seems you are still keen on purple, though these days go for muted hues rather than the bold statements of old. Has your writing, I wonder, gone a similar way?

Even when I mentioned my visit to the island, you looked blank. I kept my voice down. It would have been crass to broadcast our acquaintanceship to a roomful of name-spotters and gossipmongers. I asked about your husband – let's call him Angus. Your smile was brittle. Perhaps he is no longer, or is no longer your husband.

I didn't mention that, earlier in the week, I was seated at a very similar table, signing copies of my own new novel – historical crime with a broad vein of romance – and treading a fine line between affable chitchat and keeping the queue moving. Nor did I add that I'd been allocated a considerably larger venue. You held a book open at the title page with a tobacco-stained forefinger. I might not have noticed the staining were I still a smoker.

Do you want a dedication?

Behind me, emitting small sighs of worshipful anticipation, a handful of stragglers shuffled closer. I'd resigned myself to a wait, made a point of hanging back and joining what appeared to be the end of the queue so that when my turn came, I wouldn't hold up the proceedings by engaging you in conversation.

No, I said. Just a signature.

I hadn't intended to sound so abrupt but there it is. You scrawled your somewhat famous name, snapped the book shut and looked me straight in the eye.

Here you are. Nice to meet you. Goodbye.

You dismissed me with a brisk handshake and turned on the charm for whoever was next in line.

I didn't leave immediately. I moved closer to the bookshelves and stood in a pool of chagrin and indecision, sweat from my palms leaching into the classy dust jacket of my signed copy. I thought I might try to catch another quick word when the queue fizzled out and the manager released you, but I was too slow to make my move: a clutch of local press swooped, no doubt intending to whisk you off to the nearest pub and pump you for quotes. I wasn't about to butt in on that cabal: they know me well enough but pick and choose when to acknowledge the fact. It was time to go, while I still had some wind in my sails.

A few months after our lunch, at your invitation, I was your houseguest. By coincidence, I was researching a novel set on the northerly archipelago where you've made your home, planning to intertwine stories set in different social groups and historical periods. There was plenty of choice: Neolithic communities, Viking invaders, Greenlandic whalers, Italian prisoners of war. And, more recently, there were people like you, who wanted to escape the rat race and urban grit, and bake their own bread in a wood-burning stove. My book, as it happens, did quite well. I'm sure I asked my publisher to send you a copy but whether it reached you is anybody's guess.

To my urban eyes, your island life was close to a rural idyll: your house, built from reclaimed local stone, was spacious, warm and bright – all that the original buildings were not; a herd of sleek black goats provided milk and a soft, salty cheese; the walled garden (restored by Angus) provided fruit and vegetables; there was decent fishing off the point.

The plan was that I'd stay with you for three nights then catch the ferry to a smaller, archaeologically important island, but the morning after what was to have been my last, sweet evening on the terrace, a furious storm struck. We could see it coming, moving over the water like a vast black bird. All ferries were cancelled until further notice. Angus rounded up the goats, herded them into the shed then went to inspect the barn – from which he ran a small press – for leaks. There were none.

Angus took great care over everything, especially his books, for which he put quality and design over profit every time. He specialised in island history, mythology, flora and fauna. He published your early novels but when your career took off, he insisted you move to a more commercially viable publisher. I still have your first novel – signed, of course, and dedicated: To my friend – ah, but that would be telling. And a handsomely illustrated book on island mosses.

I offered to sit out the storm in the B&B by the terminal but you wouldn't hear of it. You had work to do but *surely* I could amuse myself – I distinctly remember your emphasis – and Angus might appreciate some help with the bread-making. Predictably, Angus was particular about his bread and would finesse each of my rounds of dough before setting aside to prove. Down the corridor, you clacked away on your typewriter.

The weather was too rough to venture out of doors without good reason. Mostly, I kept to my room. I read about the ingenuity of Neolithic construction and the significance of incident light, about Viking farming methods and social structures, about plunderers, press-gangs and prisoners of war. I made notes. I dozed. It was like being in a pleasant period of convalescence: no pain, no discomfort, only strict instructions to take it easy.

I compared the runes knitted into the band of a hat I'd bought on the ferry with a facsimile of the original. The seller had told me they translated as 'many a woman has walked stooping in here' but Angus pointed out that 'walked' could just as easily have been 'worked': 'many a woman has worked stooping in here', and 'stooping' could have been 'stopping' or 'stepping'. I didn't know it at the time but Angus's commentary was a gift: ultimately, *stooping, working women* became central to my Viking story. I still have the hat: the island wool is virtually indestructible.

In the evenings, we ate, drank, smoked and talked around the kitchen table. Angus spoke of a legendary storm in the nineteenth century. Some say it scoured the coastline so violently that a stone-age settlement, hitherto buried for millennia, was laid bare. You spoke of your aim to become fully self-sufficient. When I praised your simple, flavoursome food, you dismissed my compliments, with some irritation: *The taste doesn't matter. What matters is that we produced it ourselves.* Angus was more gracious.

After three days the storm blew itself out. The wind had heaped sand and earth all along the back wall of the garden and plants were strewn around like casualties: snapped, flattened, half-buried. The rosemary bush, however, had survived and after the rain was sharply scented. Angus sighed, and went to fetch a rake. You lit another cigarette. I offered to stick around and help with the damage as best I could but you were adamant that I should leave as soon as possible. The ferries were running again but on a skeleton service. There was one later that morning. As I'd been pretty much packed since before the storm hit, it took no time at all to gather my remaining things together. In watery sunshine, I made my way along Windblown Bay to the ferry terminal. You waved from the gate.

It is getting light and the birds are chirping intermittently. I wrap my signed copy of your book in a sheet of tissue and place it on the dresser. It goes against the grain to spend good money on a book then abandon it when I've barely made a start but I won't revisit it. So much more to read – and to write. The annual charity auction is the next event in our literary calendar. The organisers are always on the lookout for signed copies, and something by you – while you're still all the rage – should fetch a decent price.

Yours, &C.

Wolfskin

It was the end of a long, bitter winter. Easter was only a couple of weeks away and dirty old snow still covered the ground. A black wolf had got into farmer Grass's henhouse and through hunger, fear and a rush of adrenalin brought on by the taste of blood, had run amok, nipping and biting at random, terrifying the hens out of their fluttering wits. Grass, a top-heavy man with hands like shovels, had lumbered into the henhouse, picked up his gun and without a moment's hesitation shot the wolf.

Our entire lunchtime conversation was taken up with the wolf shooting. My sisters, who had witnessed the event, ate and blabbed and were told off for talking with their mouths full. They interrupted each other's action replays of all the squawking and snarling, the feathers floating free of the chicken wire, the shots fired. Soon after the cracks of gunfire had been consumed by the still noon air – one sister insisted there were three shots, the other four – Grass emerged from the henhouse, dragging the dripping carcass by the tail. To spontaneous applause from the assembled children, he crossed the yard, shouldered his way into his barn and let the door bang behind him. He left a broad smear of blood on the dirty snow. As there was nothing else to see at this point, and because it was lunchtime, I conclude that most of the audience drifted off, including my sisters, who were always hungry and keen to spread news.

My appetite for dumpling soup was diminished by my sisters' protracted descriptions of the shootout in the henhouse but hunger won the day and, a little more slowly than normal, I cleared my plate. Immediately after lunch they dragged me, protesting, to the site of the morning's drama. But it was all over now, wasn't it? There wouldn't be anything more to see, I whined in vain. By the time we reached the barn, a clutch of other children had already bolted down their lunch and reassembled.

He's been in there the whole time.

He didn't go for lunch.

How do you know if you went home for yours?

My dad said.

How would your dad know if he was having his lunch? Has he got X-ray eyes?

His dad's got cross eyes. And squint teeth.

Has not!

Crisscross eyes and a mouth like a bag of clothes pegs.

A fight would have started there and then had Grass not emerged from the barn with a look of serious intent on his florid face, and a puffed-up air of importance. The wolfskin, still with head, feet and tail attached, was slung round his shoulders like a bloody cape. We had an idea of what was going to happen. We had heard tell of the ritual, the charm against further calamity. We had heard tell but never seen it.

Grass hammered. We children hung back, whispering

and nudging each other, trying but failing to contain their
excitement. When he had driven the final nail into the tail
of the wolfskin, the surface area now appeared much larger
than when it had encased three dimensions of flesh and bone.
Farmer Grass stepped back, checked that the nails were firmly
in place, wiped a gout of blood from his brow with a sleeve
of his straw-flecked jersey, then returned to the farmhouse,
presumably to eat his lunch, amid our gasps of awe.

My sisters – and most of the other children present – were
quivering with excitement at the opportunity to inspect the
wolfskin at close quarters: to stroke or tug the thick, dark fur,
to count the teeth and claws, to poke an explorative finger
into the bloody bullet wound or dare a whole small hand
between the gaping jaws.

Despite the inevitable taunts and charges of cowardice,
I kept my distance from the poking and prodding, the mock
disgust and unabashed gloating. But I was there too, in body
and soul. Oh yes. Just not so vociferous, not so candid.
Perhaps I had my reasons, perhaps not.

Even now, when our childhood has become a distant
country, if my sisters wish to remind me of their superior
bravery or curiosity, all they need to do is mention farmer
Grass. My memory of that day stops at the barn door, at
the shaggy pelt with its clumps of matted hair and congealing
blood, spread-eagled on raw, weathered wood: a dark, heart-
stopping star.

Bottled Lives

The last time you saw Viki, the very last time, you'd gone
to meet her after one of her anatomy classes. The medical
school, a nautilus of mediaeval chambers, was the one of the
few remaining jewels in the cracked crown of a city ravaged
by war and hastily, cheaply rebuilt. The school turned in on
itself: a prized survivor, an anachronism, anomaly, it had been
spared the indignity of being subsumed by the forest of brave
new tower blocks which conformed to Stalinist specifications.
In the low-ceilinged corridors brass fitments and wooden
wainscotting gleamed darkly. On the walls hung portraits
of famous medics, prints of ground-breaking treatments in
the field and cartoons depicting the drastic practices of the
profession before it knew better.

After many winding corridors, in the dark heart of the
building you found the place and waited outside the closed,
ancient door. The sonorous summation of a lecture leaked

into the stale air of the corridor, then the rumble and scrape of students rising to their feet and pushing back chairs. The door swung open and the professor brushed past you and made off down the corridor, abrupt and listing, as if his shoes pinched or his joints protested. The class followed at a respectful distance, chatting at a low pitch, patting pockets for cigarettes and matches.

Viki squeezed your hand briefly then let go. You were careful. Mostly.

Wait, she said. Let them go on.

When the others had turned a corner and the voices had faded away to nothing, she pulled you into the anatomy room, closed the door and pressed herself against you. Her hair smelled of gherkin-scented, state-issue shampoo.

I shouldn't even be in here! you said, disengaging from her embrace.

There's no sign to say it's against the rules.

No sign doesn't mean no rule.

The room was spacious, high-ceilinged and bright, with two narrow rows of glass panelling in the roof and a narrow gallery. Around the walls, glass cabinets housed rows of specimen bottles. Sunlight cut through the skylight panels and glanced off the cabinets, splitting into what you called rainbows and Viki called spectral bands. The acoustics were such that the sound of your footsteps crossing the linoleum swelled briefly and then was cut dead.

Sepia and cream, umber and gold, the anatomy room was a confluence of the medical and the ecclesiastical. Skeletons occupied alcoves, like hanging saints. Viki, eyes bright and eager, pulled you from one exhibit to another. At first you only looked to please her. A liver, its ventricles dyed for demonstration purposes, glowed like a blue, denuded tree.

A flayed foot, in butcher meat hues, revealed the intricate interplay between muscles and sinew. Eyeballs and scrotal sacs, hearts, lungs and brains displayed various stages of development or deterioration. But it was the embryos and stillborns, the bottled lives which never were or were never meant to be, that stopped your breath: an encephalitic foetus, its head pressed against the glass as it might have been inside the womb, a Cyclops, its only features a rosebud mouth and perfect single eye, conjoined twins whose pained eyes could never meet each other's gaze. Deep under the skin of existence, where explanations weren't required and ideology was superfluous, you lost track of time, forgot how little of it you and Viki still had together. Viki placed her hand over yours and pressed both against the glass, leaving a ten-digit imprint.

There, she said.

On the seventeenth floor of a twenty-storey block, from the window of Viki's student accommodation, was the best possible view. Or the worst. The border fence was only thirty yards away and you could see far into the other and, yes, greener side.

I can't make up my mind whether I love the view or hate it, said Viki.

It was late afternoon in early autumn, a clear day. You could see for miles. The sun gilded the frills of pillowy clouds, its rays fanning down to the western horizon; the scene was as sublime as a Renaissance painting; all that was missing were clusters of chubby *putti*.

You played a favourite game. It was your turn to ask the questions.

You're driving that blue car down a tree-lined avenue. The chrome fenders catch the light.

I see it.

Where do you live?

I live in an apartment overlooking the river.

Describe the apartment.

Big and bright. It's on two floors and overlooks a clean, quiet street at the front. At the back is a garden, more trees, a river.

Favourite room?

The bedroom but the bedroom is private.

Next favourite room.

The living room. The walls are pale blue. A vast sofa sits in front of a broad bay window. There are tall plants. In big blue pots. Deep blue. Prussian blue! The leaves of the plants glisten as if they've just been misted. The light is soft and warm. This is a happy house, one in which plants thrive. The ambience is good. For a city the air is excellent. The living room is at the back of the house, overlooking slender gold-leaved trees and a river flowing behind them, a slow, clean river. On a hot day fish jump, fat, heavy fish, scales glinting as they catch the light. There are no steel works or towerblocks in sight. There is no toxic grit in the air, no pollution.

What kind of work do you do?

I'm a specialist in sports injuries. I run a clinic for athletes. It's the best clinic in the country.

How much do you earn?

Lots. Too much. In all kinds of currencies.

Do you live alone?

No.

Who lives with you?

My beloved.

Who is your beloved?

She is a very famous and successful filmmaker whose work has received international recognition.

And so on. Sometimes Viki was a heart surgeon, sometimes she was in a lab, at the cutting edge of immunology research.

When she wasn't in the mood for worthy careers, she was a plastic surgeon tending the rich and already beautiful. As for you, if you were not a film-maker, you were an artist, a pop star, a fashion or furniture designer, more often than not something lightweight, frivolous.

The two of you always shared a bright, spacious home. You were always successful and wealthy, and enjoyed glamorous pastimes and exotic holidays. Either you had a vibrant social life or were so devoted to your careers and each other that there was neither the time in your lives nor the need for anybody else. That night the game was no different.

Facing each other, you remained standing at the window, soaking up the last of the sun, and each other, Viki's arms looping your waist, clasped in the small of your back. You undressed each other, slowly bared yourselves to the sky and each other, as if there were all the time in the world. Anybody who might have observed you – though to discern any detail would have required military-strength binoculars – was in another country with its own laws and lawbreakers to attend to. In your last shared moments you were exposed, yet impregnable.

That evening – and what a lovely evening it was – you were sad but also somehow impatient to get on with your sadness. You wanted to hold Viki forever and yet, in prolonging the moment, you couldn't ignore a dragging sense of pointlessness. Eventually you had to hurry down the stairs. The lift had broken. Again. Taking so many flights of stairs at a lick made your head spin.

You sprinted to the station and only just caught the train which would take you back to your mother's village. People called the train the Needle's Eye. Because it began its journey on the other side, the border guards were up and down the corridors all night, doing spot searches and passport checks.

The train was busy but you found a space in a six-seater compartment. The other passengers, three men and two women, were a bulky, sullen bunch: they flipped their eyelids open to see who'd come in, then flipped them shut again. You had too much leaving on your mind to care about the lack of companionship: you had left Viki and soon you would be leaving your family, your country: life as you knew it.

The compartment was dim and hushed, in the close, oppressive manner of night trains. When the guards barged in they were, as usual, rude, brusquely shaking shoulders and demanding papers, tossing torch beams around, poking at luggage and barking stupid questions. Your companions responded patiently, politely. Their politeness was unusual but you thought nothing of it at the time. When the guards moved on, accompanied by needless slamming of doors, small, wary smiles passed around the compartment.

When the noise of footsteps in the corridor died down, the man next to you drew the curtain across the window overlooking the corridor and jammed the door shut. Immediately everybody stood up and began to undress. The men removed jackets, shirts, trousers, the women lifted skirts and jerseys and you discovered what had made them all so bulky: beneath their outer garments they were each wearing – or had strapped around their torsos – several pairs of denim jeans. Once they had removed the jeans they dressed again, their skirts and trousers now hanging loosely on them. The man at the door gathered up the contraband and stuffed it into a large bag.

You did not see anything, he said, his pitted face looming too close, his breath sour from drink.

I did not see anything and I did not hear anything, you said.

I was asleep. It was the night train.

Very good, he said, patting my shoulder, grinning. You like American jeans?

No, you said.

Pity, he said. I could give you a good price for them.

As the train was pulling into the next station, the man with the bag slipped into the corridor, raised the latch on the nearest external door, dropped onto the tracks and disappeared into the night. While the train stood at the station, everybody who remained in the compartment sat still and alert, primed for another visitation from the border guards but after a couple of strained but uneventful moments the flag came down, the whistle blew and the train trundled out of the station.

How far are you going? said the woman next to you.

Two more stops.

Not far, then, she said. She was friendly now, complicit.

Without her denim padding she was thin, with the creased, leathery skin of people who work the land. Around your mother's age, maybe, she too might well have reason to hate trains, but there she was, on the Needle's Eye, probably not for the first time, supplementing her income by smuggling decadent western jeans. If she had been caught, the anti-state activity could have put her in prison – but who, then, didn't take risks?'

Your sin was of omission. You've tried to convince yourself that what you did – what you didn't do – was accidental, that in the amorous heat of your final moments together, you simply forgot to mention to Viki that Marga, your zealous sister, had found out about your anti-state predilections. Simply forgot! How could you have forgotten? And even if you

had forgotten in the heat of the moment, from your new, if
not altogether happy life of exile, you could have written. You
could have found a way to get the message past the censors
that your sister was a state snitch. It wasn't that you hadn't
learned how to say one thing and mean another, after all, but
somehow the presence of mind, the sense of urgency deserted
you. You were far away, striving to build a life for yourself, to
forge a career in a country, and an industry, where to slow
down is to be left behind.

You'd like to think that somewhere deep in Marga's dutiful,
state-serving psyche, by having Viki followed the night she
took some girl back to her high room with a view of the free
world, your sister was demonstrating misplaced sibling loyalty.
You'd like to think her actions were motivated by something
as innocent and misguided as that. Maybe one day you and
Marga will come face to face, drink tea or something together,
effect some kind of sobbing, heart-rending reconciliation. Who
knows. But like others who stayed, who endured, Marga has
many words for those who got away, most of them bitter and
foul.

When you first arrived in the free world you were dazed
by the brightness of the city by night; looped tubes of neon
advertising booze, cigarettes and strip joints leaping out from
a dark curtain of cloud and decadent, amplified music spilling
through the doors of clubs and bars: so much forbidden fruit
for the taking. The raucous noise of the city at night was alien,
addictive.

You were accustomed to quiet darkness. Not only the
country dark, not only the cold black mitt in the face of your
mother's village, the city streets were pretty damn murky as
well. You learned to listen like a lynx. Apart from shambling

drunks who tripped over broken paving stones and cracked teeth and bones in the process, most people managed to get around with whatever scant and feeble lighting was available. Street crime was almost unheard of: the penalties for such anti-state activity were the stuff of muffled whispers and deterred all but the most desperate and confused.

The city by night could be almost reassuring. People didn't have to bear witness to the bomb sites, the ugly tower blocks, the drab empty shops and bombastic slogans which shouted from hoardings and state showpieces alike. The darkness made it possible to slough the grey skin of their surroundings, to imagine a lighter, brighter life. The young imagined a brave new society with countless options and prospects, and nobody having to spend hours queuing for soap or bread or thread. The old cooked up memories of gas-lit grandeur: carriages clattering over cobbles, conveying the well-heeled to concerts and balls – and plenty: market stalls piled high with bigger cabbages, sweeter beets, fatter chickens.

One evening, not long after your official papers had eventually arrived and the family had resigned themselves to the fact that you weren't going to change your mind, you and Marga took the tram to the city centre to see a film at the state cinema. Perhaps she wanted to prove to you that you didn't need to leave home to study film, that there was plenty of home-grown talent. And so there was, but that was beside the point.

It was a close evening, threatening thunder. The tram was hot, stuffy. You can remember only snatches of what was showing though its subject, a forbidden relationship between two women, was exhilarating. At the time there was still a heavy emphasis on films which served the state and featured ordinary people making do in the face of everyday obstacles,

valiant people able to endure privation by being brimful of faith
in the wisdom, generosity and eventual flowering of the state.
You weren't convinced by the woman journalist's obsession
with the beautiful officer's wife. Rejected by the beautiful
object of her desire, the journalist then succumbed – far too
quickly – to the smouldering persistence of a heavy-browed
waitress – you didn't buy that either but no matter, the
film drove you deeper into a doomed, long-term affair with
celluloid.

The thunderstorm had played itself out while you were
in the cinema, its rumbles and crashes intruding on the
soundtrack, adding some unintentional dramatic effects. As you
picked your way through the puddles to the tramstop, Marga
was circumspect in her appraisal of the movie, commenting
only on the quality of the acting and the cinematography,
saying nothing at all about its content. You were the same.
Back then, everybody operated with approximations,
abridgements, edited versions. Careful half-truths were your
lingua franca. Careless words cost lives but what of your dire
lack of words?

When you arrived here with a letter from K, a national
luminary in the field, whose films travelled internationally even
if he didn't – and a signed affidavit that you would not become
a burden on the host country – Viki was midway through her
medical studies. She had promised that when her studying was
over she would find a way, somehow, to get out and join you.
Then the army was brought in, the borders were firmly closed
and Viki became a bird in a locked cage.

Your mother balanced her wish to have you back in the
nest with a long-standing mistrust of political movements.
One week she would write a lengthy, emotional plea that you

quit your languishing career as a film-maker and come home. The next week a one-line card would arrive saying something cryptic like: *The air is very bad here. You must think only of your health.*

Sister Marga was too busy furthering her cloak-and-dagger career to write much. Resistance was all very admirable but you couldn't eat ideology and Marga had no wish to sacrifice her youth and health and party privileges to a gulag. When she did get around to making contact, her letters were such cant that you rarely finished reading them.

And Viki's letters – those false, bright little fripperies told you to stay put. She was fine and getting on well with her studies. She would find a way out. *Patience*, she'd said. *Patience.*

You have saved all letters from home and the stamps still churn you up – their familiarity, contradictions, irrelevance. One, in naïf style, portrays a worker figure in overalls, stiff as a wooden puppet, clutching a spanner. The other features a fin-de-siècle painting of a country house in all its pre-revolutionary splendour.

Viki's final bid for freedom demonstrated beyond question that she was unable to practise what she preached, that she had run out of patience. In essence it is a filmic cliché, one which marks a point of high drama:

The audience has come to sympathise with the plight of the tragic heroine, knows that she is acting rashly, desperately, that the chance of success is negligible, yet hopes against hope that lady luck will smile, that somehow the searchlight beam will stop short of that particular patch of fence, that some distraction elsewhere will give the rash /brave /desperate young woman the few extra seconds required to scale the heights. Pluckily, she clambers up the fence, almost to the top. She appears to be doing well and the suspense mounts: the viewers are on the edge of their seats, willing the heroine to succeed in her bid for freedom... And then, of course, she is spotted, the alarm is raised, the guards approach. Dramatic music. Close-ups. Gunshots. After a final, vain attempt to scale the fence the fatally wounded young woman slumps against the wire. Saddened but not really surprised, the viewers sink back into their seats. Anybody could have predicted, if they had properly grasped the plot, that the heroine was doomed from the start.

It's doubtful that Viki actually attempted to climb the fence. Only a complete fool would have done that, given the height of it and the heavy presence of the guards. More likely she discovered a break in the fence which nobody had got around to fixing, tried to squeeze through and was shot in the process.

Perhaps it made the international papers but you didn't read the papers much. It was months before you heard, via one of your mother's cryptic notes, about Viki's *permanent detention,* and you became an exile for real. You hunched your shoulder against the world, refused company, sympathy, therapy, dropped out of college – well, no, the college dropped you. You barely noticed. Bar work paid the rent and ensured booze was readily available, as well as a menu of drugs of choice in the hospitality industry. In the small hours, when the city that never sleeps might at least have been taking a short nap, you reframed your own tragic love affair as a screenplay. Nobody wanted *Bleak Dawn.* It was the wrong time, the wrong place, the wrong mood, definitely the wrong title.

The paper is soft and yellowed with age, the typescript fuzzy. You begin to read it but after a few pages slap it back in the box file and kick it beneath the bed. You really should burn the thing, move on. It's not healthy to dwell. Does nobody any good. You could go back. Now. Things have changed a lot. You'd hardly recognise the place, all the renovations, all the free trade. Your mother would welcome you back, kill the fatted calf – or more likely piglet. She'd give you houseroom until you get back on your feet. Marga might be less open-armed but now that her own fortunes have been reversed – who knows? Whatever you do, you need to get out of this dump. It makes your skin crawl.

So long, so long, so long; no more, no more, no more.

Vanitas

It wasn't just about the money. Of course not. It was about a breach of trust, a broken agreement. About making a promise to someone and not honouring that promise and how can a struggling artist survive on broken agreements when he can barely make ends meet on honoured agreements? Yes, he should have got the contract in writing, with half the fee upfront and the other half on delivery but at the time, late at night in an upmarket hotel bar, there had seemed no need for that: the commission had come out of the blue, from a chance meeting.

It had all happened so quickly, so easily: none of the usual waiting and hoping that folks would put their money where their mouths were; none of the grovelling, the standing around while would-be patrons poked about the studio, humming and hawing over portraits of friends and family and a couple of well-known figures done on spec – and offering some artistic advice into the bargain – no, none of that. The guy, a high-flying financier, didn't even ask to visit the studio ahead of the sittings; the guy took him on trust, on his ever so slightly massaged reputation, and when a man takes you on trust it's only fair to reciprocate. Under subdued, flattering lighting, over a fine malt, with piano glissandos in the background, they'd shaken on what at the time had seemed a very good deal indeed.

The agreed fee had been generous, too good for the painter to turn down. And one commission in the world of high finance could well lead to others. If he played his cards right, he might soon have been making a tidy income from people with money to burn and vanity enough to commission a portrait in oils. But he hadn't played his cards right because when, in the board room, against a glittering backdrop of the expanding financial section of the city, the painter unveiled the finished canvas, the financier clicked his well-maintained teeth.

I don't like it, he said.

A man who knows his own mind! the painter replied with a short laugh. Lots of people don't like their portraits. But why should anybody *like* their portrait? Isn't the point to see ourselves as other see us?

It doesn't give the impression I want to convey. Can you alter it?

I'm a painter, not a bespoke tailor.

So you can't alter it?

Why should I? It's a good painting. Honest. Shows your complexity. Shrewd, steely but still with some flexibility.

I don't want it.

A benefactor of the arts should embrace artistic freedom.

I don't pay for what I don't want.

What d'you mean you don't want it? You asked me to

make it. What am I supposed to do with it if you don't want it? If we'd been talking about a rock star or even a minor TV celebrity, I might have found another buyer but who in their right mind would want a picture of you on their living room wall?

That's not my concern, said the financier, and before things became too heated, summoned a security officer who escorted the painter off the premises.

The painter had boasted about this commission. It had been a while since he'd had anything to boast about and had arranged to celebrate with a bunch of fellow artists. Now what would he tell them? It wasn't right. It wasn't fair. He'd been cheated and he couldn't afford to be cheated. He was a struggling artist, unlike some who were doing very well for themselves. He had spent money on materials and several months of his life on a painting – for what? He hadn't even enjoyed the process. All the guy had talked about during the sittings was golf and the deals he'd cut in St Andrews and Carnoustie. He'd got the likeness all right: cold and calculating, just what you'd expect of someone who'd made an obscene amount of money. He'd considered softening the mouth to offset the gimlet eyes but that, he reckoned, would have been cheating. He dumped the painting in his studio and made for the bar.

The painter was too angry to keep his bad news to himself. Some of his mates related similar tales of woe – of commissions that had fallen through, galleries which had let them down. Others urged him to sue, to strike a blow for badly treated artists everywhere. He should consider not just *actual* loss but *potential* loss. How many future commissions *might* have rested on the back of that one, that foot in the door, that lucky break? How many days, weeks, had he worked for nothing? And what of the psychological damage? How long might it take him to regain his self-confidence? Considered in this light, the amount of damage which the painter felt he had suffered was ballooning.

The junior partner in the firm of solicitors agreed that it was an unfortunate situation but advised against litigation. The painter's adversary was a seasoned player in legal matters. Without a written contract, the risk was considerable. But wasn't it a risk worth taking? Wouldn't the case get publicity and wasn't all publicity good publicity? The solicitor's job was to act on his client's behalf and didn't he, the client, have a genuine grievance? A case might be made, the junior partner agreed, but the outcome could not be guaranteed. How much in damages did he wish to claim?

It's not just about the money, it's about fair play – and my reputation, said the painter, then named a figure which would either make him a rich man, or, if proceedings dragged on (which they did), if he refused a generous, out of court settlement (which he did, and then increased his claim), and legal fees mounted steadily (which they did), would undoubtedly ruin him.

EFEMERI

It is Sunday evening and Alyssa has spent an energetic day in bed with her new boyfriend. At least she thinks of Lars as her boyfriend, though she has only met him twice before, both times on a Sunday. She has decided that from now on she will only meet him on Sundays because she likes to keep things clear and simple, and to know what's happening when.

So he's good in bed but is he on the level? asks Moll. They are in the staff changing rooms, tying back their hair, buttoning up their uniforms.

I can see right through him, says Alyssa.

You shouldn't take your work home with you.

I can't help it, says Alyssa.

Sometimes it's okay not to know, to pretend everything's fine.

Not for me, says Alyssa.

No, says Moll, maybe not.

Alyssa is incapable of pretence and due to her inability to offer praise where it isn't due, she goes through boyfriends fast. As far as sex goes she certainly won't say she's done when she isn't. Lars has copious sexual stamina despite being skinny as a stick insect; Alyssa sees this as a plus.

After they've been through the staff security checks, Moll and Alyssa click their tooled-up belts into place and make their way across the processing hall to the checkpoints. The vast glass building is an echo chamber of squeaking trolley wheels and rumbling walkways against a never-ending backtrack of bleeps. The queues are long and slow-moving. The air is stale, heavy.

There's Leon, says Moll. Gate nine. He's looking good.

No he isn't, says Alyssa. He's looking as fake as ever.

Leon Bass, the division controller, is in his early fifties. He has a meaty swagger, a mane of freshly highlighted gold-brown hair and a habit of tossing his head like a lion about to roar. Leon likes to live up to his name though roaring, rumour has it, he confines to the bedroom. In a work situation, a low growl usually suffices.

Come on, Alyssa. Don't spoil my sex-with-the-boss fantasy. It helps me get through the night shift.

Doing your job properly will help you more.

What's bugging you?

I don't know. Yet.

Keep me posted.

Maybe I will, maybe I won't.

Alyssa has a problem with the truth: she can't avoid it. People on the receiving end of her bald pronouncements find her rude, brutal. Alyssa won't mince her words. She won't bite her tongue. She will say exactly what she thinks, when she thinks it, and can't comprehend why jaws drop in shock, shame or outrage.

Leon clocks Moll and Alyssa and gives them a brisk little salute.

Why, says Alyssa, would you want to have sex with that grizzled old git? You'd be better off paying for a robobonk. No risk of infection and guaranteed to last the pace.

It's a fantasy, says Moll. A mind game.

Fantasies are pointless. Unless you can eventually act them out.

As usual, Alyssa strides across the concourse, followed by Moll, who is shorter and stouter, and struggles to keep up. Alyssa never fails to get a buzz from entering the security halls at the beginning of her shift. She's eager to get started, to root out the liars and cheats. She likes her uniform, its epaulettes, button-down pockets, its dark, heavy-duty fabric and red piping. It makes her feel taller, more purposeful. If it weren't against the rules, she'd wear her uniform all the time.

Before they enter the processing hall, people often pause to do one last mental cleanout. Some close their eyes and do some deep breathing, as if they were about to plunge into an abyss, or turn tail and bolt back the way they came, before they pass the sensors which activate the shatterproof doors. From there on they are in the hands of the security guards.

Leon's on his way over, says Moll. How do I look?

Your eyebrows need plucking.

Do they? D'you have any tweezers?

Here? says Alyssa. Of course not.

Are they really bad?

Yeah.

In the business of false compliments, Alyssa is ahead of the game: if the new border controls, rushed through parliament after the last presidential assassination, can really be described as a game. Whereas others are finding it difficult to rethink their thoughts, to make them innocuous and transparent, Alyssa's thoughts have always been transparent, if not innocuous. In the past, her thoughts have got her into trouble; now everybody's thoughts are getting them into trouble. Especially in Alyssa's line of work.

Evening, ladies, says Leon. I trust you had a relaxing day.

I had a lovely lazy Sunday, says Moll.

I had a totally knackering day in bed, says Alyssa.

Too much information, says Leon, stretching his lips into a mirthless grin, then moving on to inspect staff changeover all the way down the line.

Alyssa enjoys her work and is considered to be one of the best. She can pick up on the slightest flicker of irregularity, is shit-hot on body language but what really sets her apart from the others is that old, disputed and unquantifiable chestnut: intuition. Given the spectacular advances in psychological profiling and neuroscience, Alyssa's reliance on being guided by a hunch is considered a hokey throwback, irrational and irrelevant as a rabbit's foot or a red sky at night.

After the day staff have logged out from Gate thirteen – where the functional magnetic resonance imaging (FMRI) scanner is located – Moll and Alyssa key in their ID codes and signal to the first in line to step inside the cubicle. There's always a bit of hassle when the shifts change, especially at Gate thirteen. Those who have been singled out to go through 'EFEMERI' – as security staff have tagged the scanner – are tetchy enough without having to be kept waiting. Rumours go around that some guards are easier to get past than others, that some have a price. The rumours are true.

Neuroimaging at border controls is still cumbersome and costly: as yet it is only used for spot checks, a mixture

of random and overtly suspicious characters, but the leaders
are calling for the scanning of all travellers, and research
into developing cheaper, more compact scanners is ongoing.
The decimated human rights movement is opposed to this
development. *Our thoughts are our own!* the campaigners cry,
though even the most ardent of them know that the battle has
already been lost.

Many religious groups, on the other hand, including Moll's
all-singing, all-dancing ecumenical church – support the use of
neuroimaging. Some consider it a godsend: a sin contemplated
is no less than a sin enacted; prevention is better than cure.
But what of those whose brains contain the most dangerous
thoughts, who wipe them clean on a regular basis? The more
people have to hide, the greater lengths they will go to hide it.

Moll and Alyssa's first case of the evening is a distracted-
looking woman in her mid-sixties. It may be the gin she reeks
of which makes her eyes pop and her words run away with
her:

It's so long since I've travelled. I don't know how many
years it is now but the last time I crossed the border was
before independence. I did vote for independence but I
didn't expect all this extra fuss just because I want to visit my
grandchildren south of the border. That's surely not a crime,
is it?

Step this way, please, ma'am, says Alyssa.

Is something the matter? Is something showing up on
your screen? Can you really tell exactly what I'm thinking
right at this moment? I bet you can't. I bet you can't really tell
anything at all from all those fancy images. I bet it's all a trick,
to intimidate people, to put people off travelling; that's what it
is, isn't it?

The woman casts around, hoping for support from others

in the queue but everybody just looks bored and irritated by the time she's wasting. Alyssa sighs loudly and pointedly. Moll scrunches together her untidy eyebrows.

Nothing's the matter, ma'am. Stand still, please. And don't speak until the questions come up on the screen. And then you should answer *briefly*. You do know what that means?

Of course I do, slurs the woman. I wasn't born yesterday.

No, says Alyssa. You were born sixty-five years, three months and seventeen days ago.

Pshhhhh! Didn't anybody ever tell you that a lady's age is her secret?

We don't do secrets here. Pass.

Is that it? Can I go?

Pass through the doorway, ma'am. Immediately.

The woman flounces off, tutting and blowing out her cheeks.

Next.

Well in advance of travelling, people prepare for the checkpoints. Encephalic modification clinics offer innovative hippocampal procedures and claim high success rates, at a price. If the top end of the modification market is beyond your funds, there are other avenues to explore: a wide range of drugs available over and under the counter; traditional therapies like meditation, hypnotism, yoga and juggling; puzzles and tasks geared towards cognitive realignment; a smörgåsbord of dietary regimes.

Alyssa prefers the night shift. How people behave when they are half-asleep and disorientated is more interesting than their daytime selves, their guard is down; they forget to approach the barriers wearing determined, forthright expressions; they don't try to curry favour with chummy comments about how hard the guards work, etcetera. Alyssa has no time for pointless chit-chat.

It has been a shift much like any other: a few awkward
customers, a few idiots, wise guys, drama queens, pains in
the arse, a few anxious souls with nothing to hide convinced
that EFEMERI would pick up some imaginary thought crime.
Towards the end of the shift, as day is beginning to break
and the processing centre becomes infused with rosy dawn
light, Alyssa is distracted by a nearby commotion. A lanky
young man in an eccentric, anachronistic get-up involving a
deerstalker, spats and goggles which date back to the early
days of flying machines is refusing to remove his eyewear and
twirling a Malacca cane in a reckless manner.

     If you don't do as you're told, sir, says Leon, you will be
refused passage.

     My good fellow, says lanky young man, in an affected,
antiquated manner. Who *do* you think you're talking to?

     I don't care who I'm talking to, says Leon, his voice deep
and thick and threatening. You do what you're told or you
stop right here.

     You jest. Indeed you do. I've had my fill of this *bagatelle* of
a country.

     Leon's face goes dark: he's a dyed-in-the-wool nationalist.
He buzzes for back-up and immediately a phalanx of armed
guards approaches.

     Gate thirteen, sir. Move along if you know what's good for
you.

     My dear chap, are threats part of your code of practice?

     There are heavy fines for obstructing officers in carrying
out their duties. And plenty witnesses who'll say you're doing
exactly that.

     Oh, very well then, says the young man, whose name is

Brenn. Do your worst! Scrutinize the catacombs of my grey matter. I assure you, you'll find nothing amiss.

The silly grin on his face might suggest that Brenn is high on some mood enhancer but up close Alyssa sees a clear, challenging glint in his eye. He's planned to be picked out, to subject himself to EFEMERI.

So this is your truth machine, is it? says Brenn. Oh, the wonders of science! To spy on the most private domains of *homo sapiens*. What progress we've made! Now everybody's secret self can be revealed. We've killed off mystery once and for all. And what good will come of it?

Step inside, sir, if you please.

My pleasure entirely.

Leon nods to Moll and Alyssa. It's a nod that means: give him the works. Which they do. Moll goes through the full version of the questionnaire. Section headings include: purpose of visit; contacts at destination; physical and mental health; sexual orientation; religious and political affiliations; alcohol and drug consumption; education and social background; leisure activities; languages spoken; history of previous travel.

Alyssa checks the screen as Brenn responds to each area of questioning. Not a flicker. His brain waves are as consistent as stitches on a sewing machine.

He's clean, Moll keys into the textbox which only she and Alyssa can see.

No, Alyssa replies. Know in my bones.

Passed all. Bones not evidence.

Brenn emerges from the capsule, his grin still intact.

Did you find me interesting, ladies? Did you find my answers revealing?

Wait there, sir, says Alyssa.

She buzzes for Leon, who is standing nearby with the

guards, picking out more candidates for Gate thirteen.

So? says Leon.

Room V, says Alyssa. Moll looks askance. Room V, Alyssa repeats.

My, my, says Brenn. First Gate thirteen and now Room V!

Come this way, says Leon.

Brenn is escorted to the interrogation room. Alyssa is struck by his bravado, his arrogance, his bare-faced cheek. He has been relieved of his cane and flying goggles but seems all the more amused by the proceedings, as if this development has also been part of his plan. His jaunty walk reminds her of Lars, whom she last saw a few hours earlier, fresh from the shower, a tiny towel wrapped modestly around his waist. When she asked what Lars would be doing while she was at work, he told her that he was going to visit his mother. It was a regular arrangement. She'd cook him dinner and pour out her woes over the roast chicken and gravy. Alyssa believes Lars. She doesn't believe Brenn.

Alyssa becomes restless. She'd like to see what's happening in the interrogation room but only upper-level security deals with the background checks, the up close and personal intimidation, the mind games. How will Brenn fare and why is he putting himself through this ordeal?

Alyssa was one of the first to volunteer for user testing and blazed through the tests. This didn't make her popular with her colleagues. *We're not going anywhere*, they whined. *We stay here and watch people go in and out. What we think about doesn't matter.* But of course it does. EFEMERI is only as good as the person observing the results. There's always a permissible margin of error, a rise or dip in the readings which is open to interpretation.

We should call Leon for this one, Moll keys into their

private text box.

The woman in question is middle-aged, well-dressed, tight-lipped. There are concerns over her place of origin and her final destination. She has language problems and her scores on politics and gender issues are over the limit.

No, Alyssa replies. Clean.

You blind?

Not the bigger picture.

Calling Leon. End of.

But Moll doesn't have to call Leon because he is already approaching the gate with Brenn ambling freely beside him. No guards and Brenn is even more bumptious than before, twirling his damn cane and swivelling his goggled head like some street entertainer. People are laughing. There's even some tentative applause.

Let him pass, says Leon. And Alyssa – my office after your shift.

Farewell, my lovelies! Brenn declares, practically prancing through Gate thirteen, blowing Alyssa and Moll a kiss as he continues towards the exit, and the freedom to do whatever it is that he has planned.

Fugue

She has been drawn towards the intangibility of darkness like temptation itself, has wrapped it around her like a sorcerer's cloak, concealed herself in its nebulous drift. Invisibility has invigorated her, put a spring in her step, led her up the literal garden path to the stubborn gate, which squealed and grated as she dragged it open. As if a pack of stray dogs might have seized the opportunity to mooch unchecked in the muddy beds of her garden or to defecate on her doorstep, she scraped the gate shut at her back. Streetlamps cast saucers of milky light on the pavement.

If anyone noticed this gaunt, muffled-up woman they would have assumed that she knew where she was going, that she had an assignation, a destination, that somebody at the other end was, without anxiety, anticipating her arrival. She has walked and walked at a determined, monotonous pace: not fast enough to have given the impression that she was in flight from anything real or imagined; not slow enough to have been described as a nocturnal stravaig.

Due to her lack of haste an observer would have assumed that nothing untoward had befallen her or any nearest and dearest, that she was neither on her way to seek urgent help nor responding to a request for the same; had that been the case, would she not, after all, have taken a taxi or, at the very least, struck out with intent?

Due to the absence of any break in her stride or any observable shilly-shallying as she approached crossroads, roundabouts, junctions and forking paths, an observer would have assumed that this dogged, all but invisible woman knew very well where she was going. Our hypothetical observer would have been wrong.

For several hours now this gaunt, *distrait* woman who has cast her glance this way and that in a mechanical and unresponsive way, whose crossed forearms have been clamped to her ribcage as if to prevent some incarcerated thing from breaking-free, has been moving further and further from her garden flat in the city centre.

How long she has been walking she could not say. Where she has come from she could not say either. She has forgotten where she lives, forgotten why she left her flat at such a late hour. Of the route she has taken, she has no recollection. She could not tell you the last thing she noticed, the last sound she heard. Her mind is not empty; it is busy, furiously, dangerously busy but she cannot recall a single thought, a single idea she has had since she shut her door.

Wrapped in darkness and layers of warm, non-reflective clothing, her throbbing feet and the now distant city lights are indications that she has been on the move for several hours but she does not make these connections. She does not make

any connection between then and now. A body in motion, she
continues.

From the garden gate to the pillar box, past the dense
privet hedges which surround the convent, she has walked.
Every weekday the convent provides freshly prepared food for
a shifting band of homeless folk – the Little Sisters of Mercy
would never refer to their diners as *shiftless* – but at night the
convent is deeply still and deeply silent: the nuns are either
praying or sleeping the sleep of the charitable.

From the convent past the Sacred Heart Chapel, from
the thumping, blacked-out windows of the lap-dancing joint
to the striplit glare of the 24/7 convenience store, from here
to there, from there to the next place, she has only broken
her stride to avoid oncoming traffic or to obey the red man's
raised hand. The headlights of passing cars have flared in her
face then faded. To the drivers of the cars, she has registered
as little more than a faint, moving shadow.

It has been a clear, cold night. Pelts of frost glittered on
railings, lampposts, parked cars. Our gaunt, persistent woman
has sniffed the air as if she might ingest some information from
the sweet notes and the spicy, the sour and the foul. Some
smells, in particular the combination of hops and coal dust,
have transported her instantaneously to a younger version
of herself, to a time in her life when roaming the city at night
meant independence, a rendezvous, a possible adventure.
But these scenes from the past have no sooner presented
themselves than they've gone; bubbles of memory burst one
after the other.

She has slipped through dark throngs on city centre
thoroughfares, maintaining the same steady pace, her body in
continuous motion, her thoughts constantly erasing themselves
except for a single idea: that a *solution* might flow into the

void between one footfall and another. She is unaware of any problem that might require a solution, only that a solution must, somehow, somewhere, sometime be found.

She has left behind the shopfronts of clubs, bars and curry houses, and advanced into the subdued gloom of residential terraces, avenues, courts and crescents, where the streetlamps are dimmer and further apart, where folk keep the darkness at bay with TV or computer screen, the halo of a bedside lamp or the gleam of a nursery night light. Through gaps in curtains she has glimpsed slivers, shards, wedges of the lives of others but has come upon no solution.

She has moved outwards, from city centre tenements to terrace houses, from hunched-shoulder bungalows to flimsy new builds, from blocky council estates to the ragged edges of the city where the darkness is hollow, windblown and hostile.

The further she is from the city, where there are more hills and woods than houses, the deeper the darkness becomes. Only creatures with night vision can observe her now: cats, foxes, owls. She can hear her own footsteps on pavement and muddy path, hear her breath, her pulse, the grinding of her teeth; she can hear small scrabblings, hoots and howls, dead leaves dropping from trees, branches creaking. She is becoming part of the darkness, becoming nobody, nothing. No more in time, in no time at all, she is finally, uneasily, beside herself. It can't last.

The Green Wings of Hope

Esperança does not live in hope, though her eyes are the same opaque green as the small winged beetle that is her namesake. Hope involves looking forward, beyond the moment, into the future, and Esperança no longer looks into the future.

Nor does she look to the past. When she first came here, to the great city, with the great Christ on top of the mountain raising his great arms to the sky, she was forever looking over her shoulder, casting quick green glances behind her, the way she did as a child, trying to catch her shadow on the hop, skittering on dirt roads or ballooning against adobe walls, up to mischief.

Here no shadow sticks to the non-slip soles of her ugly practical shoes. Esperança lives in a place lit 24/7, where the light casts no shadows. She lives in a place that never sleeps and wall clocks tell the time across the globe. Knowing the time in Tokyo or London makes her feel calm, connected. At the end of her shift, someone thousands of miles west, just like her, is starting her shift and someone else, thousands of miles east is, if she's lucky, already deep in sleep.

In her green nylon overalls, Esperança trundles a cart stacked with toilet rolls and soap dispenser refills, with bleach and disinfectant, rags and scrubbing brushes, rubber gloves. She is invisible to those she services: travellers with holdalls and backpacks, suitcases and handbags who just can't wait to use the facilities to attend to the calls of nature and freshen up, to apply their duty-free lipstick and scoosh on some perfume from a glass bottle in the shape of a flower, a beautiful woman.

Esperança lives indoors, in a temperature-controlled environment, in perpetual artificial light. Oh, there are a few dark corners, broom cupboards, store rooms where she might take a catnap. When she's brazen, she sleeps on the concourse, on the metal benches, alongside young travellers, on their way to discover the world or on their way home to sleep in a soft bed after having seen how others live.

Esperança might be brazen but she is not foolhardy. In a toilet cubicle, she'll strip off her uniform, rinse it in the hand basin, blow it dry under a roaring Dyson Air Blade which sounds like an emergency but does the job, then stow it in her bag. In the morning, before the sun comes up, she might take advantage of the public showers to attend to other laundry and matters of personal hygiene.

Sometimes she feels anxious. Sleeping on the premises is against the rules for staff but when she's out of uniform her boss doesn't know her, the rest of the cleaning squad has learned to leave her be and travellers don't care what rules she is breaking as long as she's quiet, as long as she doesn't scream out and slash the air in her sleep, as long as the green wings of hope remain tucked away and Esperança is content to remain in the perpetual moment.

Night Ward

This is the moment Ava has come to hate: when the mother
gull, a flapping shadow against the dusk, arcs away and
Deeptha, the charge nurse, closes the curtains on the outside
world. When she is satisfied that no light can sneak in through
any chink, Deeptha adjusts Gussie's sleep mask.

It ain't workin! It ain't bleedin workin! Gussie snaps
through her plastic visor.

That's because you keep messing around with it! Deeptha
snaps back. I've sorted it – *again* – so leave it be, will you.
Leave it be!

What you sayin? I can't hear what you're sayin!

Gussie is in the bed directly across from Ava, bolt upright
as usual. She is ninety-nine, which she'll announce to anyone
within earshot, selectively deaf, selectively gaga, and selectively
incapable of doing anything for herself.

As if to underline that night mode has commenced and
she expects her *ladies* to behave accordingly, Deeptha pads
emphatically down the ward to its ever-open door, flips off
the lights and leaves. It's ten-thirty, and the ward, with its

buzzers, bleeping monitors, its whistling snores, grunts, howls
and wails is like some dim, grim amusement arcade. For Ava,
lights out heralds the long haul till dawn, the hours on end of
sleeplessness.

By day, having a bed by the window more than compensates
for the distance to the facilities, though there's not much of a
view: a low-rise block, a ribbon of sky, a family of gulls. A pair
of puffed-up chicks, as yet unable to fly, occupy the roof ridge.
Periodically, the mother bird drops out of the blue to poke
titbits into the gaping gullets of her young. After feeding time
comes family time: a nudgy, step-we-gaily along the ridge. Ava
hardly ever *hears* the birds: as soon as a window is opened and
soft summer air touches her cheek, somebody begins to bleat
about being cold, and keeps on bleating until the window is
once again shut.

The ward has been named after a nearby coastal town,
and the mural in the corridor is a jolly splash of buckets,
spades, sandcastles and stripy deckchairs but the cheer stops
at the door: few of Deeptha's *ladies* will dip their toes in the
sea again. Will Ava be one of the lucky ones? She flexes her
bad hand, splaying and clenching numb fingers. She aims for
a hundred flexes but loses count, enthusiasm. For several
minutes she is transfixed by the second-hand circling the wall
clock.

Tonight, all but one of the eight beds are filled, though
occupancy can change in a heartbeat – or, as often as not,
in the absence of one. To Ava's right is Grace, delivered not
long after Ava by Danny the porter. So far, Grace – chiselled
cheekbones, long neck, a tumble of dark curls – hasn't opened
her eyes. Sometimes she mutters and there's distress in her
muttering, but it's a subdued distress that disturbs nobody and

so remains under the nurses' radar. She hasn't responded to
any inducements to eat or drink. Nor to repeated requests
to cover up her legs, which isn't surprising in someone who's
comatose. Ava reckons the nurses are making a fuss about
nothing. Grace's legs are slender, lightly freckled, free from
lesions, easily the least troubling body parts on show.

Mary-Belle is diagonally opposite – *kitty-corner,* to use
the bastardised American term. If Ava owned a decent
smartphone, instead of the beat-up old thing with as faulty a
memory as Gussie, Googling the origins of *kitty-corner* might
have eaten up a morsel of the looming night. But all that's
available to her is idle, pointless speculation. In the five days
and nights Ava has been in the ward – and which feel so much
longer – Mary-Belle hasn't uttered a peep nor moved a muscle.
Twice a day, to prevent bed sores, the nurses roll her from
one side to the other. Otherwise, she's log-rigid, eyes tight
shut, mouth agape. The only indication that Mary-Belle is still
among the living is the trace on her vital signs display.

One bed down from Grace is Jinny, a timid skelf of a
woman. The bed next to Mary-Belle is empty. Nearest the
door are Pam and Margot. Pam has no legs but suffers her
trials with equanimity and has no truck with anyone who
doesn't. Like Margot. Just after the prissy, supercilious male
nurse had dished out the meds, Margot threw a wobbler. She
must have known the nurses had something nasty in store as
she was shrieking before they'd got their sleeves rolled up.

Ava never did get acquainted with the last occupant of the
empty bed, a bald, gloomy woman with clay-grey skin. In the
small hours – two nights ago, three? – Ava woke to a hushed
kerfuffle around the bald woman's bed. The curtains were
swished closed. Wordlessly, in long, lugubrious strides, Danny
came and went. When the curtains swished open again, the

bed had been remade and the woman was gone, so utterly
gone it was as if she'd never been there. There are few sights
as desolate as a recently vacated hospital bed: the narrow
mattress, the tight envelope of industrially laundered linen.

Despite her full-face mask, Gussie is the noisiest sleeper,
honking and snorting away like billy-o. Jinny whimpers,
apologetically. Margot wails, unapologetically. Grace mutters.
She has a deep, posh, smoker's voice. She flings her pretty legs
around. Every so often, somebody calls, shrieks, bawls for the
nurses. The nurses rarely come. They have better things to do,
better places to be: out the back, for instance, snatching a fag
in the bushes among the looping bats and blowing plumes of
smoke into the night air. If they're indoors, and there's nothing
urgent, they're at their station, doing a bit of admin and taking
their sweet time about it, because on the night shift they can,
chatting and laughing all the while. Uproariously. Whatever do
night nurses find so funny?

Ava is considering another trip to the toilet. She has been
going more often than she really needs to go but she's finished
her book and doesn't have enough battery for her phone radio
– how else is she to pass the time? It's not as if she's disturbing
anybody. She's ever so quiet, and the castors on the portable
IV don't squeak at all as she tiptoes to and fro. Besides, as
she's the only one in the ward who can make the toilets
unaided, she may as well make the most of the opportunity.
For the others it's the bedpan, the commode or, if they're
lucky, a supported stagger. The nurses have made it quite clear
that they'd sooner trundle in the commode.

Gussie is talking in her sleep. She swings between replaying
the day's dust-ups with doctors, nurses and visitors, and re-
enacting some highly charged scenario from her distant past.
When she's in the zone – a place of fog, shadows, the slap of

river water on stone and tense, rushed whispers – all the gruff, sweary petulance she assails the ward with by day evaporates:

Take blankets, food, water. Essentials only. A torch. Don't forget a torch. Batteries. Don't forget batteries. When you get there, you might have to wait a bit. Wait quietly, calmly. Once you're admitted, find a space on the floor quick as you can and settle down. Don't make a fuss. Don't attract attention. Keep your own counsel. If somebody speaks to you, nod, smile. But say nothing. Don't meet anybody's gaze for long. If anybody starts asking questions, move on, find another spot. Don't ask anybody for anything. Bide your time –

Gussie's voice fades, as if she is being drawn backwards down a long tunnel. Her blaring snores resume.

Ava rolls onto her bad side, places both feet on the floor. Everything's fine, she tells herself. There's nothing wrong with the bad foot, the bad leg, hip, ribcage, shoulder. Her brain is just delivering the wrong messages. She loops the IV tube around the stand, grips the handles and sets off, putting all her energy into appearing as balanced and symmetrical as she can. Not that anybody is paying attention.

Grace snuffles, stretches, waggles her head. Mary-Belle is out cold. Will Mary-Belle, *can* she ever emerge from such depths of torpor? Jinny, flat on her back, submits to a personal horror show playing out on the ward ceiling. Margot wails intermittently, claws the air. Wrapped in the beam of her bedlight, Pam is sitting up, reading calmly. Her dark, bobbed hair is freshly brushed and even from several beds away it's evident that she's wearing lipstick – fire-engine red. It's half an hour to midnight. The ward is populated by sick old women. It's the weekend. Unless there's an emergency, the patients won't see a doctor until the start of the week – so why is Pam dolled-up?

The corridor is bright and empty. Out of sight, a phone

rings, stops; a kettle comes to the boil, clicks off. A female
nurse hoots with laughter, falls silent. Ava steers herself
and her IV into the toilet, locks the door and after several
awkward manoeuvres pees negligibly. The cubicle is warm and
fairly clean. While she's contemplating her peaky, bedraggled
reflection in the full-length mirror, there's a flurry of activity
in the corridor: brisk footsteps, Danny's trademark wheeze,
the squeak of trolley wheels. Is Danny delivering a new patient,
or has he come to ferry a corpse to the morgue? To avoid
the possibility of meeting death face to face, Ava loiters, until
curiosity gets the better of her and she returns, stealthily, to
the ward.

The curtains have been drawn around the empty bed and
busy shadows balloon across them. Dunts and thuds, crackle
of polyester. A running commentary, with every word as clear
as day.

Danny (cheery): Right, Paula, I'm just going to slide you
thisaway.

Ange (veteran nurse with a trace of an Irish accent): Tuck
that arm in, lovely, that's it – easy now, easy does it.

Danny: In a jiffy we'll have you snug as a bug in a rug.

Paula (new, as-yet-unseen patient, in a penetrating
monotone): I don't want to be snug as a bug! In a rug or out of
a rug!

Deeptha: The more fuss you make, Paula, the longer this is
going to take.

Paula: For all I care, it can take till kingdom come.

Deeptha: Don't expect us to stick around, then. Some of us
have homes to go to.

Paula: Aren't you the lucky ones. I used to have a home but
they took it from me. They took –

Danny: Whoa! Mind how you go, Paula. We can't have you

falling out of bed, can we?

Paula: I don't care.

Ange: Easy now, lovely. Let us do what we're here for.

Paula: They stole it. They stole my home!

Deeptha: Who did? Who stole your home?

Paula: Your lot. YOUR LOT!

Deeptha: People are trying to sleep, Paula.

Paula: I don't give a tuppenny fuck.

Deeptha: We'll have none of that language in here, thank you.

Paula: I can say what I like. You can't stop me –

Ange: All done, lovely.

Paula: I didn't ask to be here. I don't want to be here.

Deeptha: You don't have any choice, my dear. Like it or lump it.

Deeptha opens the curtains. Danny, doleful and dishevelled as ever, reverses his trolley, turns it around. As he passes her bed, Pam, coquettish, tilts her head and bestows on him a fire-engine red smile. Has Pam got the hots for Danny?

Ange straightens her coke-bottle glasses. Margot stirs, moans.

Nurse! Nurse!

Go to sleep, Margot, says Deeptha.

Yes, says Pam, snapping her book shut. Go to sleep, Margot, and give the rest of us a fighting chance to do the same.

But nurse! wails Margot. NURRRRRSSSSSE!

With brief, backward glances, Deeptha and Ange leave.

Grace mutters. Gussie honks. Paula, slowly, scans the room, her gaze coming to rest on Jinny.

What's *your* name? she says.

Jinny pulls a blanket over her head.

What you doing *that* for? You'll *suffocate*. What's your name? WHAT'S YOUR NAME?

D'you think, says Pam, you could just shut up?

Why should I? says Paula.

Because, nitwit, it's the middle of the bloody night.

I'm not a nitwit. *You're* a nitwit. A twit. A piece of twiddle. Piece of piddle. Piece of pimp. Piece of pimple. Pie. Pimple pie. Pigeon pie. Piebald pie. A piece of pigsty –

I take it back, says Pam. You're not a nitwit. You're a fucking nutjob.

I'm not a nutjob –

Yes, you fucking are! And don't say, *You're the one who's a nutjob.* I am in full possession of my faculties, which is more than I can say for anybody else in here. You should be in the psych ward but d'you know why you're not? Because the psych ward's short of beds, so they brought you in here.

Paula starts up a low drone which she keeps going until the alarm on Mary-Belle's monitor goes off and the display lights start to flash. Ange and Deeptha return at a trot and sequester Mary-Belle behind gently billowing curtains. Rapid, unseen activity. Urgent whispering. This time the nurses mean to keep whatever they're saying to themselves. Surprisingly quickly, a doctor appears – young, lanky, drawn from overwork – and slips between the curtains. Hot on his heels is Danny, who halts his trolley in the central aisle. Paula swivels her head in his direction.

Did somebody die? she says. Did somebody kick the bucket?

Danny scratches his chin, says nothing.

Why won't you tell me what's going on?

Because I don't know, Paula, says Danny. Through a gap in the curtains, a hand beckons. That's me now, he says, advancing with his trolley.

Will I die? says Paula. Will I?

Who cares? says Pam.

The dunts and thuds of a body being manhandled continue until the curtains are whisked open and Danny wheels Mary-Belle away, at speed. The doctor departs, also at speed. Deeptha and Ange straighten up Mary-Belle's bed.

Did she die? says Paula. Did that old woman die?

It's not your business, says Deeptha, but no, Mary-Belle had a seizure. She is being taken for assessment.

Is she coming back? says Paula.

You'll have to wait and see, says Deeptha, and exits with Ange.

During a brief lull, the 1960s circuitry hums and there's a scrabbling in the skirting boards. Ava knows the cause of the scrabbling. She has seen the nimble hospital rats cavorting in broad daylight.

OOOOOH! OOOOOOOH! yells Gussie. NURRRRRSE! NURRRRRRRSE! I NEED TO GO! I NEED TO GO! HURRY! HURRY!

Gussie continues to yell, stabs at her call button. It is some time before Deeptha reappears, followed, too late, by Ange with a bedpan. More drawing of curtains. More remonstrations. More noises off.

Ava alternates between covering her ears and her nose; it is not possible to do both at the same time. If she had charge on her phone, she might have drowned out the noise with some Miles Davis but his *Sketches of Spain* couldn't have done anything about the smell.

Ange and Deeptha hoist Gussie, boulder-like, onto her chair, strip down and remake the bed, do much the same with the patient, deodorise the air. All the while, Gussie seesaws between obstreperousness and ingratiation:

Bugger off! Don't you effin dare! – oh, you're ever so good to me! Such wonderful gels. When I get home, I'll send you a lovely box of chocolates – Gerroff!

Once Gussie is reunited with her sleep mask, another spell of peace ensues but it is short-lived: Gussie has set the others off. Pam is next to summon the nurse. With queenly cordiality, she converses with Ange about hairstyles and makeup while she endures the indignity of the bedpan. Then it's Jinny's turn. Jinny refuses the commode point-blank; begs to be helped to the toilet.

Please, Deeptha. *Please!*

Against her better judgement, Deeptha agrees, and the two hirple across the lino, Jinny's thin fingers clutching Deeptha's sturdy forearm.

I can see you! Paula calls after them. Are you going to the toilet? I want to go too. I want to go too!

You can't, says Deeptha. You can't walk.

She can't walk either, says Paula. Look at her. She's all floppy, like Raggedy Ann. You're just about carrying her.

But I'm *not* carrying her, says Deeptha. And I'm certainly not going to carry *you*.

You could give me a piggyback.

I could not.

Piggyback. Pygmy. Pigsty. Pigtail.

What rubbish comes out of that mouth of yours, says Deeptha, as she and Jinny venture into the corridor.

Pigswill. Pigfish. Pigshit. I want to go too.

Press your call button, Paula. One of the other nurses will attend to you.

Grace is muttering.

Gussie resumes her wartime drama:

They like to come at dawn, when nobody's around to see what they're up to, when everybody is tucked up in bed and it takes longer to make a getaway. They like to catch you unawares, on the hop, so be prepared. One step ahead. You never know the moment –

If a nurse don't come and take me to the toilet, says Paula, loud and clear and staring straight at Ava, I'm going to kill you all. KILL YOU ALL. And then I might kill myself.

Tell you what, says Pam. Why don't you just kill yourself right now and put the rest of us out of our fucking misery.

I don't want to put you out of your misery. I want to KILL YOU. Nurse! calls Paula. Nurse!

Ange sweeps in, marches over to Paula's bed, folds her wiry arms. It occurs to Ava that Ange's head of ash-blonde bubble curls is a wig.

You rang. What d'you want, then?

I'm going to pee the bed, says Paula. I'm going to pee the bed and poo the bed and you'll have to change the sheets and clean up all the mess.

I'd better fetch the bedpan, then, hadn't I? Ange about-turns, marches off.

Help! Help! squeals Margot, galvanised by Ange's clicking footsteps. Save me!

They can't hear you, says Paula airily. Nobody can hear you, you stupid old cow. And even if they *can* hear you, they won't come. And even if they *do* come, they can't save you. *Nobody* can save you. I'm going to kill you. I'M GOING TO KILL EVERYBODY IN THE WARD!

Margot, somehow, stifles a sob. Jinny swallows a whimper. Ava takes slow, silent breaths. Even the bedside monitors seem quelled. The warm, stale air pulsates. Paula is bedbound, and unlikely to have the capacity to carry out her threat, unless she has managed to smuggle in some kind of missile. Even so. Even so. It is three a.m..

Well! says Grace, opening her eyes, wiggling her toes, pulling her knees up to her chin, hoisting herself up, elegantly, on an elbow.

Gimme a cigarette, she says to no-one in particular. And a gin. A large gin.

You're not allowed to smoke, says Paula.

Who says? says Grace. *You*? Who the fuck are *you*?

The human, mechanical and electronic sounds of the ward swell and ebb. There are still hours until morning when, if the night passes without Paula carrying out her threat or any other incident, Deeptha will open the curtains and let the daylight stream in. She will complete her paperwork, consign her charges to the brash, vigorous day shift then plough down the arterial corridors to the exit. If she catches her bus, and if the bus is not running late, she will reach home in just enough time to see her husband off to work, and ensure that her children eat before they leave for school. She will shower off the night shift, make herself tea and toast then lie down to sleep, in sheets which hold traces of her husband's scent.

There are still hours before the mother gull will return to feed her young, and the breakfast trolley will do the rounds. Ava regards the dim ward with wide-eyed exhaustion. It is never, of course, completely dark; the doorway remains a bright slab of light – torment for the bedbound, magnet for the mobile. It's time to make another trip to the facilities: not because she *has* to but because she can. And, also, because hospital toilets are fitted with alarm systems – and locks on the doors.

Acknowledgements

A number of these stories have previously appeared in: *The European Short Story Network*, 2012 (under the title 'Music for a While' at http://www.theshortstory.eu/); *Gutter* 1, 6 and 11; *Edinburgh Review* 130 and 141; *Scottish Review of Books* Vol 6, Issue 1, 2010 and online May 20, 2019; *Causeway* (Aberdeen University Press, 2017); *I am Because you Are* (Freight Books, 2015); *The Scotsman; Flash Magazine; New Writing Scotland* 31; *Interlitq*, August 28, 2020; *Biopunk: Stories from the Far Side of Research* (Comma Press, 2014); *Uncanny Bodies* (Luna Press, 2020), *The Art of Being Dangerous*, (Leuven University Press, 2021).

DILYS ROSE lives in Edinburgh and is a novelist, short story writer and poet. She has published twelve books, most recently *Unspeakable* (Freight, 2017), a fact-based historical novel, and a poetry pamphlet, *Stone the Crows* (Mariscat Press, 2020). *Sea Fret* is her sixth collection of short stories.